ALYS OF ASGARD

CATHERINE BANKS

Alys of Asgard by Catherine Banks

Turbo Kitten Industries™

P.O. Box 5012

Galt, CA 95632

Catherine Banks

www.catherinebanks.com

CHAPTER ONE

"Sif, stop hitting her!" Sigyn yelled as the beautiful and angry Aesir goddess punched me in the sides again and again. If she didn't stop soon my ribs would break.

"She shouldn't be here," Sif growled. "She's not one of us."

"I don't want to be like you," I growled at her. "You're a rude and cold-hearted witch."

She pried my arms apart, exposing my face which I had been protecting, and growled in my face looking more feral than ever before. "I could kill you right now, mortal."

"Odin wouldn't let you," I told her smugly. "And you'd get in trouble."

Her lip twitched in a snarl and before I could move she head butted me in the face. My nose felt like it exploded and I could feel the hot blood dripping down my face. "Ah!" I screamed in pain and tried my hardest to get her off of me. She was too strong. If only I wasn't mortal. If I were a goddess too, I would put her in her place. Then again, the reason she was attacking me was because I wasn't a goddess.

"Alys!" Thor yelled, running over and knocking Sif off of me. His hair was like golden silk and his blue eyes were as deep as the oceans on Midgard. He sat me up and tore off his shirt to wad it up against my nose. If only I didn't have to tilt my head back to stop the bloodflow, I could have looked at him shirtless a bit longer. "Can you walk?" he asked me.

"Stop protecting her!" Sif yelled at him. "She's mortal. She's supposed to get hurt!"

"You are a member of the Aesir!" He snapped at her. "Show a little more class and stop hurting her because you can. We are supposed to protect them, not purposefully hurt them."

She glared at me once more and then stormed away. Sigyn looked at me apologetically and then followed after Sif. "Thank you," I whispered. "Again." He seemed to always have to save me from one thing or another. Lately it was Sif more and more often. She and I had a terrible amount of animosity between us and it didn't seem likely to be quelled any time soon.

He ran a hand down my hair and asked, "What did you say to anger her this time?"

I turned away from him and stormed away with my fists clenched at my sides. "Nothing." I couldn't tell him what was said because that would mean admitting to him that I liked him. I couldn't admit my feelings to him.

He followed me and I found his presence incredibly reassuring. "She could kill you very easily," he reminded me.

"I don't need you to remind me of that," I snapped. "I'm well aware of my limitations." I was reminded every day that I wasn't a god and that I could be killed by them with barely a flick of their fingers.

"Alys," Jord said in shock, "Why are you bleeding?" I hadn't even seen the goddess in front of me due to my anger. She was the most gorgeous goddess on Asgard, they were all beautiful, but Jord was by far the most beautiful, and had the kindest heart of them all.

"Sif broke her nose," Thor told her.

They both knew it was a lie since Jord had healed me, but thankfully they quieted.

Loki pulled his hand away, finished with healing me and stood up. "I'll see you later, Alys."

"Goodbye, Loki." I focused on cleaning the shirt, scrubbing the red stain that was trying very hard to remain permanent.

Thor growled and thunder shook everything around me, including the ground beneath my feet. The quake caused me to lose my footing and I fell sideways into the stream. The cold water swirled up around me, tugging me along by the current, and chilled my fingers and body in an instant. I kicked my way to the surface and gasped air in as soon as my mouth was above water.

"Alys!" Thor yelled. I opened my eyes and realized with shock that I had traveled a half mile downstream from him. I didn't remember the current being so strong or fast before. He ran to me, dove into the water, and pulled me to the shore. I held onto his neck as I regained my breath and also to take the chance to touch him. "Are you alright?" he asked me as he pet my sodden hair.

I nodded my head and gripped him harder. "I'm sorry you had to get wet."

"Well it *was* starting to get hot," he said with a laugh.

I pulled away from him and found my smile mirroring his. "You're one of a kind, Thor Odinson."

"As are you, Alys," he whispered, setting his hand against my cheek.

My heartbeat became erratic, my stomach tight with nervousness, and my cheeks reddened with embarrassment. He leaned his face closer to mine, our lips only an inch apart.

"Thor!" Odin bellowed from his throne room, his voice carrying across all of Asgard from his power.

Thor stilled, his eyes locked with mine. "I have to go."

I couldn't talk. I did figure out how to let go of him and stand up, thankfully. He put his shirt on and walked towards the castle while I stared after him, trying to remember who I was and what I was supposed to do now. He turned at the castle doors and smiled brightly at me. "Alys?"

"Yes, Thor?" I somehow answered.

"Will you meet me for breakfast tomorrow?"

Breakfast? He wanted me to eat breakfast with him? "Um, yes."

"Great. I'll see you tomorrow morning then."

"Okay."

He walked into the castle and I fell down to my knees on the wet grass. I sat there in silence for a while and then started shivering from my wet clothes. Loki was going to press me for answers if I showed up in dirty and wet clothes, so I headed home to change. My home was set apart from the others, on the far side of the castle grounds right in the center of the grass-lands. Odin had built it for me with his own two hands, not even using his powers, once I was old enough to live in a place of my own, which had been at nine years old. I still had no idea how I had come to be on Asgard, but even with Sif's constant attacks, I loved it here. I had grown up with the others and learned so much about the other worlds and the other beings. I had yet to meet anyone other than the Vanir and Aesir and no matter how much I begged Odin to let me go with them when they took the others to different worlds, I wasn't allowed to go.

I pushed open my front door and hurried inside to start a fire. My home consisted of a bed, a dresser with my clothes, a table with four chairs, one window, and a fireplace large enough to hang a pot over fire to cook. I changed clothes, setting my wet ones on the back of a chair near the fireplace to dry and then sat down in it to brush my hair while it dried as well.

Someone knocked on the door, which wasn't all that abnormal, but I rarely received visitors at my home. I rubbed my arms to try to warm my skin up again and opened the door.

"Hello," Sif said with a smirk on her stupidly beautiful face.

I leaned against the door and asked, "What do you want?"

"Is that any way to address a goddess?" she asked me, but strangely there was no anger behind it. What was she up to?

"How can I help you, Sif?" I asked her more politely. I really wasn't in the mood to argue or fight, especially when I needed to meet Loki soon.

"I came to apologize," she said.

Nothing about her smirk or demeanor suggested she was coming to apologize at all. Odin had made her apologize to me before and she had acted like she was being tortured the entire time.

"Thank you," I said and started to push the door closed.

She stuck her foot in the way and reached in to grab me in a hug.

"What are you doing?" I demanded, my heart hammering in my chest and my mouth going dry.

"Don't worry, you'll forget all about this in a moment," she whispered. A strange pressure built against my head and the house swayed as I became uncontrollably dizzy.

"Stop," I begged her as I weakly fought against her.

"It's almost over," she whispered.

"What are you doing?" I asked again as my legs grew weaker and my body sank to the ground.

"Quiet, mortal and go to sleep."

I fainted a moment later.

I OPENED my eyes and found Sif standing next to my bed with a satisfied grin on her face. "Sif, what are you doing here?"

I asked, sitting up and trying to swing my legs over the edge of my bed. The movements made me very dizzy and I felt nauseous as the room spun wildly.

"You were asleep in front of your house," she said as though she had been concerned. "I brought you inside to get you warmed up again."

"Why was I outside?" I asked softly. What was the last thing I had done? I remembered Sif and me fighting earlier and Thor had stopped her, but...then what?

"Alys, you look sick," she commented. "You mortals are so easily killed. You should just lie down and rest."

As much as I hated agreeing with her about anything, she was right that I needed to rest. I had no idea why my head felt so strange, but a good rest would most likely cure it.

"Thank you, Sif," I said since it was the first time she had ever been kind to me.

She smiled and walked out of my house with a skip in her step. "Don't mention it," she said, "you just rest up."

She closed the door and I pulled my covers up around myself tighter. Why was I so cold and tired? What had I done after the fight with Sif? And why was the goddess being so kind to me all of a sudden?

CHAPTER TWO

The next afternoon I felt much better and took a stroll around Asgard, picking flowers to put in a vase inside my home. I was humming and dancing my way through one of the many flower fields when Loki appeared next to me.

"Good afternoon, Loki," I greeted him warmly. "How are you this day?"

He scowled at me and looked at the flowers in my hands. "Who are those for?"

"Myself," I answered honestly. "I wanted to add some to the vase in my home."

"What did you do last night?" he asked me with a clenched jaw. Why did he seem upset? I hadn't done anything that should have upset him. What was wrong with me picking flowers?

"I slept all night and most of this morning," I admitted.

"Slept?" he asked with worry. "Are you sick?"

I shrugged.

"Alys," Thor called as he approached us, his jaw and fists clenched when he saw Loki. "Where have you been?"

I looked at him in confusion. "What do you mean? I was just walking the fields collecting flowers."

"Where were you this morning?" he asked. "Were you with *him?*"

"And what if she was?" Loki asked with a smug smile.

"Whoa guys, calm down. Thor, I was sleeping. I just told Loki that I slept all night and most of this morning. I only woke up about an hour ago."

"What?" Thor asked in shock. "Are you ill?"

Déjà vu.

"I'm not sure," I admitted. "It's possible, but I don't understand where I would have gotten an illness from." None of the gods got sick. It was possible one of the gods had traveled to Midgard and brought a germ back with them, but no one had traveled to Midgard in a year or more.

"Did you eat?" Loki asked me.

I shook my head. "No, I just slept."

"Would you like to come with me and get something to eat?" Loki asked with a sweet smile. It was rare that he looked so sweet and kind and I noticed that he looked that way more and more when with me. It was slightly terrifying. Most of my shock was because he had asked me to eat with him. He had never done that before.

"You can't honestly want to ditch me to go with him?" Thor asked as his hands balled into fists.

"What?" I asked him. What was he talking about?

"I invited you for breakfast this morning," he told me.

"No, you didn't." I would have remembered that.

"Yes, I did."

"I invited her for supper and she didn't show up, so I should get the first meal with her," Loki said.

"Wait, what? When did you ask me for supper? I don't remember any of this," I said in exasperation. How could I have forgotten them asking me to share meals with them? That was a memory I would definitely want to have.

"I asked you yesterday when you were at the stream with him," Loki explained.

"I didn't go to the stream," I whispered and clutched at my head as it began throbbing.

"Yes, you did. We went to the stream and you were washing my shirt because it had your blood on it," Thor whispered as he stared at me, "and Loki showed up and healed your ribs."

"My blood? Why was I bleeding? Why did you heal my ribs?" The headache became even stronger, making me sway on my feet.

"What could have caused her to forget an entire evening?" Thor asked Loki.

Loki stared at me with a frightening anger that normally wasn't aimed at me. "What do you remember about yesterday?" he asked me instead of answering Thor.

"Sif and I got in a fight and then I don't know what happened after that. I woke up later that night in bed and Sif was there. She said she had found me outside my home asleep and brought me inside."

Loki cursed in the old language and fire crackled around his clenched fists. He was glorious when he was angry and even though it was terrible of me, I wished that I could see him in his true fury.

I started to fall and Thor caught me, resting a hand against my forehead to see if I had a fever. "I'm sorry I snapped at you earlier," Thor said.

It was no wonder they were mad at me. If I had stood them both up for meals, it made sense.

"I think we need to go talk to Sif," Loki growled.

"No, we should go see Odin," Thor said.

Loki sighed. "You always want to run to the All Father like a child. We don't need him. We can talk with Sif alone and find out what she did."

"How do you know Sif did anything?" I asked. "Maybe she really did find me outside."

"Why are you defending that witch?" Loki asked. "She takes every chance she gets to make you miserable."

"I'm just pointing out that it might not have been her doing," I said softly. I didn't want to take the one time she was nice and accuse her of doing something cruel if she really hadn't done anything. That would definitely push our animosity to a whole 'nother level.

"You're too soft-hearted," Loki accused me.

"For once, I have to agree with Loki," Thor said, looking like he had bitten into something rancid.

"I don't want to be part of you questioning her," I told them. "Plus, I'm hungry."

"Fine, let's get you something to eat and then Thor and I will speak with her later," Loki agreed.

Thor followed Loki, and I followed them both. It was the first time I had ever seen them talk to each other without trying to kill the other or starting a fight. They whispered angrily back and forth as we walked and I could imagine what a team they would make if they could only get along. The other worlds would tremble at their combined might if only they could focus on things together like this.

We walked into the castle and down the hallway to the dining hall. It was a glorious hall with high ceilings, chandeliers with candles, ornate sconces on the walls, and thick tables with benches enough to seat both the Aesir and Vanir races. It was lunch time and the room was surprisingly filled today. Most days, only about half of the gods and goddesses would gather at a time. Why were they all together today? Had something happened or was something about to happen? Sif turned around when she heard the door open and stared at the two gods and me in shock, and then glared at me with disdain.

Loki walked to an empty table, sat down, and grabbed a roll of bread to eat. Thor sat down across from him and I stood in place. Who should I sit by? It didn't matter which side I sat on because one of them would get mad, but who would be the least mad?

Odin walked over to me and clapped me on the shoulder. "How are you today, Alys?" he asked and pulled me down to the bench to sit between Loki and him.

"I'm alright," I answered vaguely and wished I could thank him for saving me from making the decision on where to sit.

He put his large calloused fingers under my chin and turned my face to look at him. "Your nose seems to be healed perfectly."

"My nose?" I asked softly. "What happened to my nose?"

"Sif broke it," Thor told me. "I gave you my shirt to stop the bleeding and we went to Jord who healed your nose and then we went to the stream so you could clean my shirt."

I didn't remember any of this. My head started hurting again and Odin's eyes glowed with anger. "Who tampered with Alys's mind?" he asked softly. The room silenced as soon as he began talking, so everyone heard him. It stayed silent. Odin stood up and lightning struck the ground in the center of the room. "WHO WAS IT!" he bellowed, making the walls shake and the ground beneath us tremble. It took all of my strength not to cower or hide under the table. I had lived with them my entire life, but still their bursts of anger were incredible and terrifying.

Still no one moved. Heimdall walked into the room, a towering man with the whitest skin of any of us and gold teeth, he was one of the most feared fighters in Asgard. I considered him a friend and visited him often just to sit with another being, not even talking. Heimdall held out a clear orb to Odin. I had only seen that orb once before and it was when Thor and Loki had lied to Odin about where they were the previous day. Somehow the orb projected past events in the air above.

"One last chance to come clean," Odin said as he took the orb from Heimdall. Still no movement. Odin whispered into the ball and then set it on the floor. It rolled to where the lightning had struck and began projecting. All eyes watched the projection and no one moved a muscle. It started with Sif and my fight, showing my nose getting broken and Thor shoving Sif off of me. Next it showed Jord healing me, Thor and me going to the stream, Loki talking to us, me falling in the stream, Thor saving me again, and then Thor almost kissing me. My face was aflame in embarrassment as several of the gods and goddesses turned to look at us. Next it showed me at home and Sif coming to my door where she used some type of magic on me that made me faint, whereupon she put me in my bed.

"I told you it was Sif," Loki said with dark tendrils of rage flittering around him.

"Sif," Odin spoke in a calm tone that only meant controlled fury, "you and I need to talk."

"Why does it matter if I erased a few hours of her memory?" she asked. "I didn't harm her. She is perfectly healthy. Why does it matter if I tested out my new powers on this mortal?"

"She is not just a mortal," Thor snapped. "She's our friend and a daughter of Asgard!"

"She is not a daughter of Asgard!" Sif bellowed, her eyes widening and a look of madness upon her face. "She is a mortal who should have never been brought here from Midgard. She belongs down there and she should be there with her own kind. She is ruining the balance of Asgard and the Aesir."

Now I understood. It was so obvious. How had I not seen this all before? Now that she said it like that, I could feel it within my core that she was completely right. Thor and Loki should have been focusing on a goddess such as Sif or Sigyn instead of me, a mortal. "I'm sorry, Sif," I whispered. "I didn't realize what my presence was doing."

"Enough," Odin said. "You are not upsetting the balance of anything. Sif is just a spoiled child who can't see past her own selfish desires."

"What do you think our lives would be like if you weren't here?" Sif asked me.

I glanced at Thor and Loki and then at Sigyn and Sif. "It wasn't my intention to divide you."

"You have. Your presence has caused the natural order of things to shift!" Sif yelled.

"That's enough!" Loki snapped. "The only thing she has done is brought to light your vile and selfish nature, Sif."

"Don't talk to me like that, Trickster."

Odin waved his hand and Sif disappeared. "She shall be punished. Mortal or not, she has no right to tamper with a person's memories and if she goes unpunished now, she might attempt to do this to one of us."

"I'm sorry," I whispered to Odin. And I truly was. I hadn't seen past my selfish desires that Sif and Sigyn were the ones who should be trying to win Loki and Thor's hearts. As much as that hurt me, I knew it to be true down to my very fiber.

"I knew the consequences of your existence here when I brought you," Odin told me. "And it is a decision I will never regret."

He might not regret it, but perhaps Sif was right about me needing to go to Midgard. Odin disappeared and everyone began talking again and eating. I should have been starving, but my stomach only ached with sorrow now. I stood up, bowed to Loki and Thor, and walked out of the dining hall.

"Alys!" Thor called after me.

I did not respond. My heart hurt, my head hurt, every fiber of my essence hurt. Instead of heading home I went to Heimdall's castle, Himinbjörg, where he watched the Bifrost and could see the other realms. He hadn't returned yet, but he had given me an open invitation to come and view the other realms whenever I wanted to. He had given me the invitation two years ago when Odin forbade me from traveling to them when they all went on adventures and trips together. I sat in a chair that he kept nearby and looked upon Midgard. The Midgardians were learning more and more things that I couldn't understand and using contraptions that were incredible. They had a device that allowed them to communicate to another across the world and one device that let them freeze an image on it and even print it out onto what they called paper.

I watched a group of teenagers walking together, talking, holding hands, and laughing. Life was so different there than here. What would it be like down there? Would I have friends? Would I have a good life if I went down there?

"You would be greatly missed if you left," Heimdall said in his gravelly voice, a mug of mead in his hand. He sat down against the wall where he had several cushions for lounging. He drank a lot of mead and the cushions were very comfortable, especially when drunk.

"She's right," I whispered as I continued to watch the teenagers all over Midgard.

"Whether she is correct about you altering the intended events of this world or not is irrelevant."

"How?" I asked, turning away from Midgard to look at him.

"You're here and the events have already transpired. Do you really think leaving now will mean Thor or Loki will want Sif? If she is the reason you leave, they will despise her for it."

He was probably right, but... "What if she isn't the reason I leave?" I asked him.

He halted with his mug halfway to his lips. "Alys, that is not what I meant."

"You have the powers of foresight. Look into the future where I go to Midgard," I begged him.

"No," he said and then took a long drink from his mug.

"Why not?" I demanded.

"Because Odin will not be pleased to find out that I did such a thing."

"Heimdall," I whined, "I need to know. Would I survive down there?" There were all kinds of things like diseases, tornadoes, and monsoons. I wasn't really sure what any of that was honestly.

"No."

"Heimdall."

"No."

"Please."

"No."

"Come on!" I begged him.

He groaned and stood up to refill his mug. "I will grant you one question, Alys of Asgard, but I will not send you to Midgard this day, no matter the answer or how the answer makes you feel."

Okay, I had to think of a good one. It had to be broad enough to get a full answer from him, he could be tricky at times, but also not so broad that his answer could mean something different. What did I want to know? I was almost positive that I could survive on Midgard, so that wasn't the question I wanted to ask. Should I ask who Thor's wife was in the future? No. Loki? No.

"Take your time," he teased me as he relaxed on the cushions again. "I have nothing else to do."

"Shh," I ordered him as I paced back and forth across the chambers.

He laughed at me and watched the other worlds while I thought.

"If I go and live on Midgard within the next year, will balance be restored to Asgard?" I asked him softly.

"This is the question you wish to ask me?" he asked, his eyes wide. "Are you certain this is the one you wish answered?"

I nodded my head. It really wasn't the question I wanted to ask, but it was the one I needed to ask. The answer would determine my course of action over the next year.

"Very well." He set his mug down, closed his eyes and began murmuring in the old language. His eyes flew open and looked like two glowing pearls. "If Alys goes to Midgard within the next year and lives there, the balance of Asgard will be restored. However, there will be consequences to the actions and payment will be necessary."

"What kind of payment and when will it be due?" I asked him.

His eyes returned to normal and he said, "You were given one question, not three."

"Thank you," I whispered, even though part of me felt terribly depressed at the confirmation.

"Perhaps it is time that Asgard is off-balance," he said softly. "It might improve matters instead of making them worse."

"I appreciate your attempts to make me feel better. You are a good friend," I told him, kissed his cheek, and headed out of Himinbjörg. The trip back to my home seemed to take an entire day and when I finally made it, the sun had long since set. I pushed open my door and was shocked to find Loki sitting at my table asleep.

I tip-toed over to him and stared at the handsome god before me. He was given such a sour welcoming at school every day that it was a wonder he even showed up. I wasn't sure why the others disliked him so much. He did like to play tricks on them, but it was never anything overly serious or dangerous. I looked at him in this vulnerable state and wished the others could see him as I did. He was simply misunderstood. I reached towards him, my fingers inching towards a lock of hair that had fallen across his face as he slept.

I was a breath away from touching it when he grabbed my arm and opened his eyes. "What are you doing?" he asked me sleepily.

"I, uh..."

"Don't lie to me," he ordered me.

"I was going to brush the hair away from your face," I admitted with flaming cheeks.

He released my wrist and dropped his hand back to his side. "Proceed."

Was he serious? He simply stared at me as if in answer. My hand was trembling now and no matter how much I tried to stop it or will it to be solid, it wouldn't. I pressed my fingertips to his forehead and slid them backwards, pushing the hair behind his ear. My heart was pounding loudly within my chest and there was no doubt he could hear it. I started to move my hand away, but he grabbed my wrist again and pulled me forward until I was sitting in his lap and his lips were on mine. I gasped in shock and he kissed me harder. His fingers became entwined in my hair and my entire body felt as though it were on fire. He leaned back, lifted my hand to his face and leaned his face against my palm. "Where have you been, Alys?"

"At Himinbjörg," I managed to answer as my heart tried its hardest to break out of my chest.

His eyes bore into mine as he asked, "What did you discuss with Heimdall?"

I had to stop touching him. I had to get away from him. "N-nothing," I stuttered as I threw myself out of his lap and to the floor. As embarrassing as the move was, it had been necessary. I stood back up and sat in the chair across the table from him before taking a bread roll from the basket I noticed on the table. He must have brought it with him for me since I hadn't eaten.

"What did you discuss with him?" he asked me again, as though I hadn't heard him the first time.

"It's a private discussion that I don't need to tell you about," I snapped. I was doing this for them. Why couldn't he see that? Why couldn't he understand that I needed to set the balance right?

He leaned forward menacingly, his eyes glowing with fury. "If you try to leave Asgard, I will hunt you down across the nine worlds," he told me with such seriousness that I almost forgot to chew the bread in my mouth.

"I'm not going anywhere." *Today at least.*

"That promise stretches for your entire lifetime and beyond," he told me.

He had never made such intense proclamations towards me before. It was a promise that showed more than anything else could just how much I meant to him. It was also confirmation that I needed to leave soon to right the balance or it might never be restored. "Your devotion terrifies me," I admitted to him.

He smirked at me and said, "Good."

I took a piece of meat from the basket and before I could ask, he took it from me, created a small flame to heat it, and then put it on a plate for me. "Thank you," I whispered before eating it.

"You're most welcome."

I finished eating and stared at the center of the table in front of me. "Loki," I whispered.

"Yes?"

I shook my head and stood up. I couldn't ask him that. I couldn't even hint that I was planning to leave in the future. I turned to face my fireplace and rubbed my hands together in front of the flames. "Thank you for being such a good friend to me."

I heard the chair scoot across the ground and then his warm arms encircled me and he rested his chin on my shoulder to whisper into my ear, "You are the one who should be thanked for their friendship. If it weren't for you, I fear the darkness that stirs in my breast would have long since taken over."

Darkness? What was he talking about? I turned around and placed my hand on the center of his chest. "Loki..."

He rested his hand on top of mine and pressed it harder into his chest. "Every time I am with you, the darkness is suppressed a bit more by the light your presence brings."

The room disappeared and I saw a well with light at the top and a swirling, inky darkness below, churning and writhing as it attempted to escape. It seemed endless and powerful beyond anything I had ever encountered. The darkness tried to push past the light, but it could not break through. I blinked and could see Loki again. "Does it hurt?" I asked him breathlessly.

"Your absence hurts far more than suppressing that darkness and dealing with its attempted escape." Slowly he leaned forward and kissed my lips tenderly. "You are my light, Alys, and without you I would be lost to that darkness."

Damn him. Damn him! He had to be lying. It had to be a trick. It was just a way for him to try to convince me to stay.

"Loki, I..."

He put his finger to my lips and said, "It is late and you have another visitor coming. I shall take my leave."

Another visitor?

"Will you dine with me tomorrow morning?" he asked. "You did stand me up twice now."

I blushed and whispered, "I'm sorry."

"Dine with me tomorrow for breakfast and all shall be forgiven."

"Okay," I said and nodded my head. It was the least I could do.

He tucked a strand of hair behind my ear and kissed my cheek. "I shall count the hours until we meet again."

Someone knocked on my door and when I looked towards it, Loki disappeared. "Who is it?" I asked breathlessly.

"Thor," he said in his deep, sexy voice.

I took a few breaths to try to calm myself and stop the blush that was present before opening the door and smiling at the God of Thunder. "Good evening," I greeted him.

"May I come in?" he requested, always the gentleman.

I opened my door farther and nodded. He walked inside and stood in front of the fireplace with his muscles clenched in his back. I shut my door and watched him in silence a moment. "How can I help you?" I asked him.

Before I could blink, he was in front of me and kissing me. His kiss was fiery and passionate and fierce. It was exactly like he was. When he pulled back, he whispered, "That was what I had intended to do at the stream."

My head spun from the kiss as I cleared my throat and tried to speak. "Uh, um, wow."

He smiled and kissed me slowly. "I tried to find you after you left, but I couldn't locate you."

"I went to Himinbjörg," I told him instead of trying to hide it from him.

His eyes widened and then he glared down at me. "No, you cannot go to Midgard. It is out of the question! Sif is just an angry and bitter girl..."

I put my hand on his cheek and kissed him to get him to stop talking. It worked and continued to work for several minutes beyond. "This is not what I expected to happen when you came in," I admitted to him.

"It is long overdue," he told me and kissed me again.

I felt bad for kissing him and Loki on the same day and just minutes apart, but I wasn't in a committed relationship to either. Truly, I wasn't in a relationship at all. That meant it was alright, didn't it? I hoped so. I still felt bad, but a larger part of me was gloating.

"I should leave," Thor whispered sadly. "It's late."

"It is late," I agreed.

He lifted me up and kissed me fiercely, making my head spin and my heart race. "Meet me for breakfast?" he asked.

"I can't," I whispered without explaining why and prayed to anyone who was listening that he didn't ask me for one.

"Lunch, then."

Phew. I nodded my head. "Okay."

He set me down and kissed my cheek with a butterfly kiss. "Good night, Alys."

"Good night, Thor."

I waited until he closed the door to throw myself onto my bed and sigh happily. Even if I left tomorrow, tonight made me the happiest mortal in all of the nine worlds.

CHAPTER THREE

I practically skipped on my way to Loki's place for breakfast, the memory of the two gods visiting me the night before still very present in my mind.

"You seem in a good mood today," Odin commented as he appeared to walk beside me.

"I am. How are you today, All Father?" I asked him with a wide smile.

"For the most part, I am well. There hasn't been war recently between the worlds, which is a blessing in itself. My family is healthy and happy. And you are growing into a very fine woman."

I wasn't sure what to say to him since I was planning to leave and somehow, I think he knew that.

"But the only negative is that there is a rumor you were discussing leaving Midgard with Heimdall."

Damn that gold-toothed god!

"It would seem you aren't happy like I thought you were," Odin continued. "And that makes me very sad."

"I am happy here," I told him with all the truthfulness I felt at that statement. Aside from realizing that I was ruining the balance here, I was happy.

"What can I do to make you even happier?" he asked me.

Create a duplicate of Loki and Thor so I don't have to ruin the balance of the Aesir? Ha! That was a wish!

I turned and smiled brightly at him. "I am happy, Odin, I swear it. There is nothing that I need here."

"What do you *want?*"

"A Pegasus?" I asked with a smirk.

"I made one once and it was an angry beast," he admitted, a distant look in his eyes as he thought about the creature. Loki had told me about the Pegasus once. It had attacked Odin and others, it's fury unprovoked and uncontrollable.

I laughed and hugged him, leaning my head against his massive chest. "I want nothing. You have given me everything that I could have ever hoped for and beyond. I am the luckiest mortal in all the realms."

"Would you be happier if I brought a mortal here for you?" he asked softly.

I jerked back from him in shock. What was he talking about? That could ruin the balance even more! "No!" I practically screamed. What would happen to Asgard if he did such a thing?

"There are many on Midgard who would kill for a chance to live here," he told me, "and I'm sure I could find one fitting to your personality and your physical appearance type."

What in Asgard was he talking about? "No, thank you. I don't think adding another mortal to this realm would be a good idea. Besides, even if they fit as you said, they might not like me."

"I think you would be hard-pressed to find someone who wouldn't like you," he said with a smirk.

"I appreciate the offer, sincerely, but I must decline."

"Very well," he said with a sigh.

After bowing to him and wishing him a good day, I hurried on my way to Loki's. He was sitting outside of his house when I arrived and smiled when I walked up to him. "Good morning," he greeted me warmly.

"Good morning."

He pushed open the door to his house and I entered without hesitation. He shut the door and then pinned me to it to kiss me. "I was worried you had forgotten about me again," he whispered and then kissed my cheek as he ran his fingertips down my throat.

"Only a fool forgets about the Trickster God," I teased him with a smirk.

"I hope you're hungry," he whispered and then kissed the left side of my neck. "I have a lot of different foods for you here," he said and kissed the right side of my neck.

"I'm famished," I said and slipped from between him and the door to find his table covered in plates of strange foods. "What is all of this?"

"These are foods from Midgard," he informed me. "These are different things they eat for breakfast."

"How did you get these?" I asked and walked around the table to survey all of the foods. They were all so different and the smells were *very* different.

He smirked at me and said, "Don't worry about that, and just enjoy yourself."

"I don't know where to start," I whispered in shock.

He picked up a round bread-looking pastry with brown and white sticky stuff spread on the top. "This is called a cinnamon roll," he explained. "Here, take a bite."

He held out the roll and I took a small bite from it. It was very sweet and delicious! "That's so good!" I exclaimed.

He smiled happily, obviously pleased with my reaction and

pulled out a chair for me to sit on. "Try this next," he said as he picked up a plate with a strange squishy-looking substance. "These are scrambled eggs."

Over the next hour I tried all of the foods he had obtained while we laughed and joked about our various reactions to the foods. Most were good, but some were strange and not something I would eat again in the future.

"I'm too full to eat another bite," I told him as I held my stomach.

He popped a fruit called a strawberry into his mouth and chewed on it while looking pleased with himself. "Was this a satisfying meal?"

"It was incredible and I really appreciate all of the effort you went to for me. Thank you, Loki." It was a very kind gesture and even if he wouldn't tell me how he had obtained all of this food, I knew it had taken him a while and a lot of planning.

"You're very welcome."

I closed my eyes as I relaxed and exhaled a loud and long happy sigh. If every day was like this, I couldn't imagine how hard it would be to force myself away from Asgard. My eyes flew open and I looked at Loki in shock. Was that why he had done it? Was he trying to convince me to stay here? Was he trying to make it hard for me to leave?

He was looking up at the ceiling with a deep frown on his face as though troubled by something. What went through the head of a god, especially one like him?

"What's wrong?" I asked him softly, completely forgetting my anger towards him.

He looked down, his eyes catching mine and he said, "Trouble is brewing and I'm afraid you might get caught up in it."

"What kind of trouble?" I asked softly. The gods were almost always fighting and the nine worlds were notorious for not getting along. That was why Odin had been happy about there being peace recently.

He stood up from his chair, walked around the table to stand beside me, and then knelt down next to me. "You need not be afraid," he told me softly. "I will do everything that I can to protect you."

"I'm not afraid for me," I told him honestly. Even being gods, it was possible for them to be killed.

He smirked and lifted my hand from my lap to rest it on his cheek. "It is very difficult for others to kill us," he told me. "You should worry more about yourself and less about us."

"Loki, what's happening?" I asked again. Just one touch from him and my heart was racing.

"War is starting," he whispered, "and I do not want you to be involved."

"Because I'm mortal?" I guessed. I knew very well that I wasn't as strong as them and it was much easier to kill me.

"Because I care about you," he whispered and then leaned up and kissed me tenderly. There was that sweet man again, the one the others never saw. Why couldn't he show them this side of himself? I knew if he showed them this side of himself that they would view him differently.

"Loki," I whispered, "Asgard is unbalanced as it is. What will war do to it now?"

He stood up angrily, turning his back to me. "You leaving us would only unbalance us more."

"Or it could give you the balance you need to ensure your survival," I whispered without looking at him.

"Do you think so little of the Aesir?" he asked me with venom in his voice, the voice he usually reserved for the other gods.

"You know that isn't it, Loki." I stood up, ready to leave and avoid this stupid fight.

He grabbed my arm and jerked me so that I spun around and faced him. "I won't let you leave," he growled in my face. "You wouldn't survive down there."

I jerked my arm back from him and said, "You don't get to order me around. I can do what I want, when I want. And I will survive wherever I go."

"Is this because of us?" he asked me softly, his harsh mask was still on despite the softness of that question.

"What do you mean?" I asked him.

"Are you trying to leave because of my advancements and my displays of affection to you?" he asked quietly, like he was afraid of someone overhearing.

I lifted my hand slowly until it rested against his cheek and said, "Not in the slightest."

"Then why do you want to leave me so badly?" he asked, leaning into my hand.

I felt tears building in my eyes and I took a shaky breath before saying, "I don't want to leave you or Asgard."

"Then don't," he whispered before kissing me roughly.

As much as I enjoyed his kiss and the thought that I could stay and be his wife, I knew that I couldn't remain here. It was going to hurt, a lot, but I had to leave Asgard within the next year. I stood in his arms for a while longer and then left with one more kiss. He watched me leave with a deep frown upon his face, furrowing his eyebrows deeper than I had ever seen before. I walked through the tall grass field, letting my hand drape behind me and the grass whisper along my palm as I began plotting my move. I walked to the arena where everyone learned to fight and practiced each day. Despite being terrible and not able to keep up with anyone, I still liked to learn and practice. I stepped into the arena and was beyond shocked to discover that it was empty. Normally there were at least two people here at any given time, even well into the night. What was happening? Where was everyone?

My worry grew, so I made my way to the castle and to the council chamber where everyone would gather for battle strategies and preparations. Thankfully, the door had been left open, so I could peek in without alerting everyone to my presence, even though Odin knew I was there immediately thanks to his powers. I peeked in and saw a table with the nine worlds drawn upon it and little carved figures of the different races placed on the worlds. Odin stood at the side of the table, scowling down at the figures and listening to Loki speaking to him. How had Loki gathered them so quickly and begun this serious topic? Had I been daydreaming so much that I had lost track of time as I went to the arena? At the far end of the room I could see Jord and several other gods and goddesses sitting in chairs in front of windows as they listened to Loki as well.

What was going on? Was he discussing the upcoming war with them? Was it that serious? I thought he meant sometime in the future, not now.

"If we don't act soon, they will launch their attack and the people of Alfheim might not survive," Loki told Odin.

"Alfheim isn't without its own army," Thor countered.

"Their army isn't strong enough to stand against the Dark Elves," Loki insisted.

"And even if Alfheim is destroyed, what does that mean for us?" Sif asked. "Why should we care if they are destroyed?"

"Because that will mean their army grows and they could set their sights on us next," Loki informed her.

"Let them come!" Tyr yelled eagerly. "They will meet their end by my blade!"

Several others cheered with him, the bloodlust running high within the Aesir.

"We won't be able to defeat them if they kill those in Alfheim and absorb their powers," Loki said over their raucous.

"Nonsense!" Tyr yelled. "We're the strongest in all of the nine worlds!"

"Only until they gain more power," Loki said, trying to get his point across.

"Since when have you been a coward?! You're usually itching for a fight?" Thor asked him.

"You're just worried for the mortal girl," Sif snapped and part of me wished to yell that I had a name. "You're worried she'll get hurt so you don't want to risk war and risk not being able to steal kisses from her."

"What?" Thor asked softly with a crackle of thunder.

"You didn't think you were the only one she was interested in, did you?" Sif asked with a mocking laugh, "Her lips have touched more than yours, Thor."

How did she know that? How did she know any of it?

"Enough!" Odin boomed, which made the walls and floors shake. I barely held myself upright and was glad I hadn't made a noise to draw attention to myself. I really didn't want everyone to see me after that little discussion.

"Please," Loki begged Odin, "I wouldn't give this advice if I wasn't certain."

"I believe you," Odin said. "As Thor said, you are usually the first one into the fray of a fight. I shall do some research and make a decision shortly. I'd really like to know where they obtained these new abilities. It's disconcerting to say the least."

Oh no, they were going to come out of the room! I ran as quietly and as quickly as I could down the hall, around the corner, left down that hall, and into the kitchen.

"What are you doing here?" Njord asked from where he was cooking himself some fish. He was the God of the Seas, fish, and wealth.

"I...came to get a snack," I said as I gasped for breath.

He looked at me skeptically a moment, but then returned to his food. I grabbed a piece of fruit from the baskets on the tables and calmed myself enough to leave and eat as I walked down the hallways. I passed by the room where everyone had been gathered to find most of them in the hallways now. Several looked at me with odd expressions, Sif glared at me, and I realized that Thor and Loki weren't there. I continued walking, needing to find Thor for lunch and headed outside.

The skies had grown dark with storm clouds and thunder boomed loudly all around me. That could only mean one thing. I hurried towards the arena where the storm seemed to be originating from and found Loki and Thor fighting. Their arms were bloody and they were fighting each other viciously. I had seen them fight before, but this was different, this fight was intense and they looked like they were seriously trying to kill each other. I had to stop them.

I had to make them stop fighting about me. I ran out into the arena and stood between them with my hands up, my palms facing each of them and yelled, "STOP!"

Lightning struck the ground behind me and a giant flame flared up in front of me, but neither harmed me.

"Are you trying to go to Hel?!" Thor demanded.

No, I didn't particularly want to visit the Goddess of the Dead yet. "Stop fighting," I ordered them, looking from Thor to Loki. "This is ridiculous."

"Is it true?" Thor asked through gritted teeth.

I knew what he was asking, but I didn't want to answer him so I turned to him and asked, "Is what true?"

"Did you kiss him?" he asked. Despite trying to look tough and angry, I could see the softness behind it and the hurt.

"Yes," I whispered.

"Why?" he asked. "Why did you kiss him and me?"

"Because I like you both," I admitted.

"She's not in a relationship with either of you, so it doesn't matter that she kissed someone else," Sigyn said from the edge of the arena.

"Sigyn," I said in shock. When had she gotten here?

"This is none of your business," Loki told her.

"I've been a terrible person," Sigyn told me. "I didn't act like your friend because I thought I had to be Sif's friend only. I should have been nicer to you and done things with you, but I didn't because I'm a fool. I'm sorry, Alys."

Where was this coming from?

"But that doesn't mean I can't help you out from time to time and right now you need a friend. You boys are so focused on your hate of each other that you can't even see what your fighting is doing to her."

The two gods turned and looked at me and I suppressed my yell of frustration. I didn't want them to know. I didn't want them to see. Why did she have to come in here and let them know?!

"She's trembling because you two almost killed her. You stupid, angry idiots barely redirected your attacks and almost killed the girl you're fighting over," she told them.

"We would never harm her," Loki told her. "Even if she was frightened by the attacks, she knows that we are in full control and that they missed because we wouldn't harm her."

"Even so, your fight is stupid. She can kiss as many boys as she wants until she gets into a committed relationship."

"That's enough," I said softly.

"Every girl deserves to be fought over, but not physically. You two should be doing your hardest to woo her and convince her that you're the one she should pick. At this rate, you're just convincing her that she should leave Asgard."

Damn her and her mouth. How did she know all of this anyways?

I turned away from all three of them and left the arena. I didn't need to stand here and deal with this. I walked a bit away and realized someone was following me. I turned around, expecting Loki or Thor, and instead found Sif. "You know I'm right," she snapped.

"I do," I said with a soft sigh. "Look, Sif, I know you're right and I've made a decision, okay? Just give me some time to plan it out thoroughly."

The look of shock on her face was priceless. "What decision did you make?" she asked.

"I'm not telling you right now. It's bad enough that you started more trouble between them today."

"They deserved to know," she said and folded her arms across her chest.

"And I deserved to be the one to tell them, in private, not in front of all of the others!" I snapped at her.

She looked down at the ground and said, "Sorry, my temper gets the better of me at times."

I blinked three times before I realized that she had indeed apologized to me and for once meant it. "You're not going to erase my memory after apologizing, are you?"

She laughed and shook her head. "No."

"Good."

"Alys," Thor called. "Come with me, please."

"I'm supposed to eat lunch with him," I explained to Sif.

"Better not keep him waiting. I don't think he'll forgive you many more times."

"Bye, Sif."

"Bye, mortal."

I walked away from her without another glance while Thor

glared at her the entire time I walked towards him. "Are you ready to eat?" I asked him.

"Yes."

"Great!" I said enthusiastically, despite not really wanting to deal with him alone at the moment.

He led the way to his room in the castle and I sat down on the window seat that looked out over the rivers of Asgard. He was the only one aside from Odin and Jord who lived in the castle. He often expressed his desire to live out of the castle walls, but he never pressed Odin about it. We had spent a lot of time in this room when we were younger, but after discovering my attraction to him I had stopped coming here. Now I felt even more nervous.

"You know I wouldn't harm you, right?" he asked me softly as he set the table, a strange habit for a warrior, but one that his mother insisted upon.

"Yes, Thor," I said as I dreamed of days when life had been simpler, when I hadn't had to worry about relationships or that I might be dooming Asgard.

"Loki told me that he thinks you're planning to leave Asgard to try to correct some imbalance you think exists," he said and then I heard a plate snap in half. I turned and saw the broken plate in his hands still.

"I know it exists, Heimdall confirmed it," I explained.

"What do you think will happen if you leave?" he asked me, finally turning to meet my gaze with lightning sparking within his eyes. I loved when they did that and wished that I could stare into them for hours and watch the lightning show of his anger.

"The balance will be restored and life will go on as it should."

"Are you unhappy here?"

"No."

"Do you think you're not worthy to be here?"

"I know I'm not."

"Why do you think that?"

"Because I am a mortal and this is the home of the Aesir."

"Don't you think Odin chose you for a reason? Don't you think that the All Father knows what he is doing? Surely you can't believe that he brought you here with no forethought."

"I think he had good intentions, but perhaps I have overstayed my welcome."

"You believe this?"

"I believe that Heimdall wouldn't lie to me and that I need to keep you all safe."

"You think by you leaving Asgard that you're going to save us somehow?" he asked me in shock.

"Yes."

"That's insanity," he spat and tossed the broken plate into the fireplace.

"The truth of the matter is that you shouldn't be dating a mortal. You should be dating a goddess."

"You want me to date someone beside you?"

I ground my teeth together angrily. "I don't *want* any of this, but it's the truth."

"And who should I date?" he asked me as he walked towards me.

"I don't know," I whispered nervously.

"Sif? Sigyn? Perhaps a Vanir?" he asked me as he walked closer and closer.

"I wouldn't presume to make a recommendation to you," I whispered.

He stopped right in front of me, lifted me up until I was eye level with him and he said, "You are the one I think about day and night. You are the one I want to kiss and can't stop thinking about kissing. Not Sigyn. Not Sif. You."

I should have stopped him, but as soon as his lips touched mine, I wrapped my arms around his neck and my legs around his waist to kiss him back. He deepened the kiss and pressed my back against the wall of his room.

"Don't leave me," he whispered. "I am not strong enough to survive your disappearance."

"You are the strongest god alive," I whispered between kisses.

"Only because I have you here with me," he whispered and kissed my throat. "Your very essence increases my strength."

"I will die very soon in your lifetime," I said sadly.

"And I will cherish every moment I have with you, mourn your death and your disappearance, and then spend every day wishing for one more second with you, for one more touch."

"Thor," I whispered in shock, "you should have children with a goddess. You should continue your lineage with powerful and strong children."

"I won't have children for another hundred years."

"You don't know that I'm the right woman for you anyways. You could decide two months from now that you can't stand the way I chew or can't stand the way I smell."

"Your smell is intoxicating, if I could bottle it I would."

My cheeks grew hot with shock and embarrassment. Why were these men admitting such feelings to me? Was it just because I was going to leave?

"And what if I left tomorrow?" I asked him softly without looking at him.

He gripped my chin with his thumb and finger and turned my head to face him. "I would find you and bring you back home. You're an Asgardian, Alys, even if you don't have powers and won't live as long as me. You are a Daughter of Asgard and I won't let you disappear from my life."

Tears were dripping from my eyes and I took a shaky breath

before saying, "I am not worthy of you or Loki, or of living here. My presence is dooming Asgard and now a threat looms that could destroy you all."

"I will vanquish it and we will celebrate together," he whispered.

I shook my head, but he kissed me deeply, stopping any more words from escaping my mouth.

CHAPTER FOUR

If I was going to run away, I had to do it when they least expected it. I also needed to decide what I would do when I got down to Midgard. I spent the next month spying on Midgard and learning how the teenagers and adults spent their time. Heimdall never spoke to me and I was perfectly fine with that. I needed to observe, not hear his cryptic phrases or have him tell me that I wouldn't survive or whatever else he might say. Thor and Loki took turns eating meals with me and spending time with me and even seemed to be getting along. Sif had been keeping her distance, and as much as I tried to keep mine from the two gods trying to date me, I couldn't do it. They were my friends and as much as it would hurt when I left, I wanted to cherish every moment I had with them.

I was fighting to stay awake one evening when Heimdall leapt up to his feet and growled, "Run home!"

I jerked myself upright, suddenly very awake, and started to run from the room, but I wasn't fast enough. A dark elf appeared in the room, having transported himself from Svartál-faheimr, and smiled at Heimdall. "I'm here to see the All

Father." I started to move again, but the elf snapped, "Stay put, mortal!"

I stopped moving and Heimdall strolled towards me slowly until he was standing between me and the elf. I couldn't control my body. Why not? Why couldn't I move? "Leave the mortal out of this. Odin is on his way here," Heimdall said with clenched fists.

"Who are you, child? Why is a mortal on Asgard?" the dark elf asked.

"That is none of your concern," Odin said when he entered the room. He looked at me, "Leave us."

I didn't need to be told twice. Odin released whatever spell had been on me and I walked out of the room slowly to show the dark elf that, with Odin there, I wasn't frightened of him and then ran as fast as I could towards my house. I made it halfway there and fell to my hands and knees to catch my breath and calm myself down. I had never met such an imposing being before. That elf had pure black eyes that held no warmth in them. I didn't doubt for a second that he would kill me if he decided to on a whim. I had been utterly powerless against him.

"Alys, what's wrong?" Loki asked me as he dropped to his knees, and placed a hand on my back. The fear was consuming me. I turned and latched onto Loki, gripping his shoulders tightly. "Shh," he cooed, "You're safe. I'm here. I'll protect you from anyone."

I couldn't speak. The eyes of the elf burned into my memory and that was all I could see, no matter if my eyes were opened or closed. He had been evil down to his core. I couldn't let that happen to Loki. If that happened to him, I didn't know what I would do.

Loki stood up with me in his arms and started walking, all the while talking to me in soothing tones and telling me over and over again that he would protect me. Could he protect me from someone like that? I couldn't bear it if he was killed protecting me. The elf had to be a dark elf because I had heard stories about other elves that were peaceful. That elf had been violence and evil incarnate.

"Alys," Loki whispered.

Did a being like that have a conscience? Or did they simply enjoy killing and felt no repercussions from their acts?

"Alys, what happened?" Loki asked me.

I realized that we were in his house, sitting in front of his fireplace with a roaring fire going and a blanket around the both of us. He must have assumed that my shivering was from cold instead of fear.

"Someone entered Asgard," I whispered. "Odin came, but he..." was petrifying. Was evil.

"Did he hurt you?" he asked through gritted teeth.

I shook my head and then turned around to bury my face against his chest. "He was terrifying," I whispered after a moment.

"You're safe, Alys. I swear I won't let anything happen to you," he whispered.

"I'm sorry," I cried with tears streaming down my face. "I'm sorry."

"Shh, you don't need to apologize for being frightened. Shh, it's alright, Alys."

"Loki, he felt so evil. He talked to me and I couldn't move. I couldn't control my body until Odin came."

"He won't lay a finger on you," he said adamantly and started to stand up.

I latched on to him and begged, "Please don't go. Please don't leave me."

He grabbed my wrists gently and I released my death grip on his shirt. "I'm not leaving you. I'm just getting you a mug of water."

"Oh." I sat down and watched as he filled a mug with water. He was acting so calm that I started to calm down myself. He handed me the mug and I drained the contents and asked for a second one, which I drained as well. "Thank you."

He sat back down and wrapped us up in the blanket again. "You don't need to thank me. I'm here for you anytime that you need me."

"Are you ever frightened of other beings?" I asked with my head on his shoulder. I took a deep breath of his scent and understood what Thor had said about wishing to bottle someone's smell.

"No, but it's good for mortals to be afraid. It will keep you alive longer," he said as he rubbed my back.

My eyelids began drooping and a yawn escaped. "Sorry, I didn't realize I was tired."

"You weren't, but I gave you a sleeping aid," he said with a laugh.

"Why?" I asked him. I knew he wasn't going to do anything bad to me. That wasn't Loki's style. He preferred you to beg him.

"I need you to stay safe, and the only way to do that right now is to make you go to sleep. Plus, this will help with your fear." He picked me up and laid me down on his bed and then covered me with blankets.

"Don't leave me," I whispered as my eyelids grew heavier by the second.

He kissed my forehead and whispered, "I will always be with you and only a second away if you call my name. Right now, I need to go ensure Asgard is safe."

"You said you wouldn't leave me," I said around a yawn.

"The Trickster must tell some fibs once in a while, most especially when it is necessary."

"Jerk," I mumbled as my eyes closed and the warmth of the bed pulled me into dreamlands.

"Sleep well, Alys."

I felt him kiss my forehead again and then he was gone.

I WOKE up with a mouth that felt like it had fabric in it and a headache. I groaned as I sat up slowly and put my head in my hands. What had happened? Where was I? I spread my fingers apart so that I could look through them and realized I was at Loki's house. Then it all came back to me. Where was he? What time was it? Was it still the same day? "Loki," I whispered hoarsely. I looked around slowly and saw the mug he had drugged me with, but didn't see any water. I started to stand up, but the drugs weren't out of my system and I fell onto something warm and fleshy.

"Why are you awake?" Loki asked me.

"How long have I been asleep?" I asked him as I lay on top of him on the floor. He must have appeared just in time to break my fall.

"Only a couple hours. Let me get you back in bed. You should sleep several more hours before this stuff wears off," he grumbled. He put me back on the bed and handed me a mug of water. I knew it was probably drugged again, but I was so thirsty that I didn't care. I took the entire mug in one gulp and then fell onto my side on the bed. He covered me again and whispered, "Don't worry, the dark elf left Asgard. You're perfectly safe."

"Good," I whispered and fell asleep again.

"ALYS!" Thor called. "Alys, wake up." Warm hands shook my body.

"I'm tired," I whispered.

"I know, but Odin wants to see you," he informed me.

I tried to open my eyes, but they wouldn't cooperate.

Thor sighed. "Fine, I'll just have to carry you."

I tried to respond, but fell asleep again.

"WAKE UP, CHILD," Odin said.

I opened my eyes and found him smiling at me. "Hello," I whispered with a sore throat.

"Here, drink this," Odin offered me a mug and I drank the contents quickly. When I had finished it I felt awake, alert, and well rested.

"Thank you," I said sincerely.

"Alys, what did that dark elf say to you before I arrived?" Odin asked.

"Um," I tried to think back, "He told me to stay where I was and then asked why a mortal was here. I think that was all."

"I told you he could sense that she was mortal," Loki said from behind me.

I turned around and realized that we were in the meeting chamber and *everyone* was here.

"How did he make you feel?" Odin asked.

"Terrified. He felt evil."

Sif snickered, but made no comment.

"Do you know why Loki gave you the sleeping potion?" Odin asked me.

I shook my head.

"Because the strongest dark elves can manipulate humans.

He could have made you walk to him or caused you to turn against one of us," Odin explained.

"I wouldn't..."

"It wouldn't be you doing it, no, but he could force you and no matter how hard you struggled, you would not be able to stop him."

"So, Loki made me go to sleep so that I didn't try to hurt anyone or so he couldn't attempt to make me hurt anyone?" I asked softly.

"Yes."

I sat numbly in the room as I took everything he had said in and then I whispered, "Is he gone?"

"Yes, I sent him away."

"Did you tell me so that I would be prepared if I saw one of them again?" I asked.

"Yes."

"Thank you."

"You're welcome. Now, why don't you go sit with the others while we discuss our upcoming strategy," Odin said.

"If it's alright with you, I would like to go to my house," I whispered to him.

"Very well," he said with a frown.

I stared at the ground and refused to meet anyone's gazes as I ran home. That dark elf could have used me to try to hurt the others. Not that I was capable of actually hurting them, but they would have had to protect themselves while attempting not to harm me. Or if it was one of the ones who didn't like me, they might hurt me just because they could get away with it. It was a terrifying thought. I couldn't imagine what would happen if I were to start attacking Thor or Loki.

I was even worse than useless, I was a huge liability. This confirmed that I needed to leave. I needed to leave soon. I didn't need to pack anything since I would just figure out things from

Midgard. If I took items, it would raise questions. I sat on my bed to wait for someone to come.

About an hour later, someone knocked on my door. I opened it and was shocked to find Sif. "I have a proposal for you," she whispered. "Can I come in?"

Part of me was worried she might attack me, but I stepped back and let her inside. She closed the door and said, "I know going to Midgard seems like it will be sad and you'll be upset about it, but what if I erase your memories before you go? That way you won't remember anything about here and you can really start over there."

I stared at her in shock and felt rage first and then, as I sat and contemplated it, I realized that it was the smartest idea I had heard and actually a very kind gesture. "Is there a way for you to leave certain memories?" I asked her.

"It depends," she said vaguely.

"Could you leave the knowledge of Midgard that I've learned the past few months?"

"Oh, yeah, easily."

"I have one more request," I whispered.

"Okay..."

"Could you figure out a phrase or word that, if said, would bring my memories back to me?" I asked softly.

"What would be the point of that? If someone accidentally said it, the memories would be back?" she asked me as though I were an imbecile.

"Please, Sif."

She sighed and said, "Fine, but I'm going to make it something complex and I'm only going to tell Odin what it is."

I nodded my head in agreement.

"When are we doing this?" she asked me.

"Tonight. Meet me at Himinbjörg at midnight."

She nodded. "Alright."

"Thank you," I whispered. "And I am sorry for upsetting the balance."

"The fact that you're willing to repair it restores your worth in my eyes."

She left the house and I plopped down on the bed to wait. I knew they would come. I just didn't know when. Now I was really glad I hadn't packed a bag. If I had items I wouldn't even know where I had gotten them from. I chewed on my fingernail as I waited nervously. Would I be able to pull this off or would they figure it out? Loki was incredibly good at reading me.

One hour.

Two hours.

Knock. Knock. Knock.

"Come in."

Loki stepped inside and I stared at the handsome god for my last time. I had to hope that his claim about the darkness wasn't true and that even with me gone, he would be able to keep somewhat behaved. He shut the door, walked to stand between my legs, and kissed me deeply. I melted into him and kissed him like it was the last time I would ever see him again, because it most likely was.

"Are you mad at me?" he asked softly and wiped the tears that had fallen down my face.

I shook my head and smiled at him. "No, I understand why you did it."

"Then why are you crying?"

"Because I could have attacked you," I whispered.

"You would never attack me," he assured me.

"If he was controlling me and I couldn't..."

He put his finger on my lips and said, "I know you. You would stop even while being controlled before trying to hurt me."

"Loki," I whispered and then pulled him forward to kiss him

again. I wished I could keep my memories, but I knew they would only cause me heartache on Midgard.

"It's late and I need to get some rest," he said as he ran his fingers through my hair.

"Okay, thank you for coming to check on me." I had known he would come, but it was still thoughtful of him.

"Will you meet me for breakfast?" he asked.

I didn't know what to say. I didn't want to lie to him and yet if I told him no, he would ask for another time and I couldn't just keep saying no. "Sure," I said with a smile.

He kissed me one last time on the lips and then once on the forehead and left my house.

I would not cry. I would not cry. I. Would. Not. Cry!

Knock. Knock. Knock.

"Come in," I said softly.

Thor poked his head in and then smiled wide. "Hi."

"Hello, Thor."

He walked in and then jumped on top of me on my bed and began to thoroughly kiss me. I had no idea how much time passed as we made out, but when he finally stopped my head was spinning. "What did I do to deserve that?" I asked him.

He laughed. "You exist."

"Well, I should exist more often," I joked.

"I can't stay," he told me as he kissed my cheeks, throat, and chin, "But I wanted to come check on you, say goodnight, and see if you would come eat dinner with me tomorrow."

"Okay," I lied.

"Great." He kissed me deeply once more and then jumped up off the bed.

"Thor," I called as he opened the door.

He stopped and turned back to me. "Thank you, for being such a good friend to me."

He smiled and winked. "Thank you for existing."

He left and I collapsed again. No crying. No crying. These men would be terrible to try to get over and I was insanely glad that Sif was going to erase my memories now. I would miss them too much if I could remember them.

I waited until just before midnight and headed to Himin-björg. I turned, looked at my home and drew in a deep breath of the night air one final time before walking inside.

Heimdall looked up at me when I entered and a deep frown creased his brow. "You're going through with this?" he asked.

I nodded my head. "It must be done."

"You know she's doing the right thing," Sif said and entered behind me.

"What is she doing here?" Heimdall asked me.

"She's helping me," I answered him vaguely.

"Are you ready?" she asked.

"Did you think of the phrase?" I asked her instead of answering.

"Yes."

"Can you put the language they speak into my head? I don't want to go down and not understand them." I hadn't even thought about it until now.

"Yes, I figured out a spell for that. I planned it out ahead of time since I knew you would need it. You'll actually just understand what people down there are saying in any of their languages and you should pick up how to speak it quickly too."

Wow, she really had planned ahead. I wasn't even sure how that was possible.

I turned and smiled at Heimdall, "Thank you for everything that you have done for me over the years."

"You are most welcome, Alys of Asgard," he said with a bow of his head.

I turned back to Sif and nodded my head. "Okay, I'm ready."

Sif placed her hands on each side of my head and closed her eyes. Pressure built within my head and then I felt like I was flying.

The pressure eased and when I opened my eyes I found a beautiful woman standing in front of me. "Uh, who are you?" I asked her curiously. I had never seen a woman so beautiful before.

She smiled and said, "I'm just a figment of your imagination, Alys. Now your dream will take you flying through a rainbow cave."

"I don't want to fly," I whispered.

She turned me around and a large very white skinned man stood over a pool of water. "Don't be afraid," she whispered in my ear. "This is only a dream, so you won't be harmed."

I wasn't sure I believed her, but what else could this be? The man smiled at me and then I was in the rainbow cave flying. It made me incredibly dizzy and I felt like I was about to throw up. Finally, my feet touched ground and as soon as I sat down I fell into blissfully dark sleep.

CHAPTER FIVE

The persistent sound of an odd bug woke me up. I opened my eyes to a white ceiling and odd smells around me. I lifted my head and stared at my strange surroundings. Where was I? The room was made of odd items and there were machines all around me.

A door opened and a woman in weird green clothes walked in. She looked up at me and smiled. "Oh, good, you're awake," she said happily.

"Wh-Where am I?" I asked her.

"You're in the hospital," she said.

"What's a hospital?" I asked. I had never heard of such a place.

"What's your name, sweetheart?"

"Alys," I whispered.

"What's your last name?"

"What do you mean? I don't have another name. It's just Alys."

"How old are you?" she asked.

"Eighteen."

"Where are your parents?"

"I don't have parents," I said.

"Where do you live?"

"I, uh, live? I don't know."

"What state are you from? Like, Utah or Idaho or California?"

What? "I don't know."

My head was pounding and I didn't understand why she was asking me all of these weird questions.

A man walked in and he smiled at me. "Hello."

"She seems to have amnesia," the woman told him.

"What's amn-amnaysa?" I asked as I rubbed my head.

"Does your head hurt?" the man asked me.

I nodded. "How did I get here?" I asked.

"Someone found you unconscious in a field and brought you in," the woman explained.

A field?

"Do you know your name?"

"Alys."

"Do you remember where you were yesterday?"

Yesterday I was... "No," I whispered in shock. What had happened? I didn't remember anything.

"It's alright," the man said. "Why don't you lay back down and rest? I'm sure you'll start remembering things soon."

I did as he asked and then stared at the strange thing in my arm. "What's this?!" I screamed in fear and started to grab it.

"No!" The woman yelled and grabbed my hands, stopping me from pulling it out. "Leave that alone. It's an IV and it's giving you fluids and medicine."

I didn't like it. Not one bit! I obeyed her, though, and lay back down to let the strange thing give me medicine.

A man in another weird outfit came in, this one had a strange gold item pinned to his chest and he seemed important somehow. "Hello, Alys, I'm Deputy Stevens."

"Hi," I whispered as he sat down in a chair beside my bed. He was attractive and seemed young to be someone important.

"The doctors here said that you didn't have any ID or any kind of identification on you when you were brought in. Do you remember anything about yourself?"

"I'm Alys and I'm eighteen."

"Anything else?" he asked.

I shook my head.

"Well, we're going to take a picture of you and see if anyone might happen to know you, okay?"

What was a picture? Would someone know me? Did I have friends who would come get me?

"Okay." He took out a strange device and held it towards me. "What is that?!" I asked in fear.

"It's a camera," he said. "It takes your picture."

"What's a picture?"

"It makes a still image of you. Here, I'll show you."

"Will it hurt?"

"No."

I didn't really believe him, but I held still and after a second he turned the device around and showed me back an image of me on the screen. "Whoa," I whispered. "That's weird."

"My grandpa refuses to use one because he thinks it is evil," he said with a laugh. "Now, I need to get your fingerprints, okay? This won't hurt either."

"Okay."

He put each finger on a strange feeling black thing and then pressed and rolled each finger on paper. Paper! I knew what paper was! He wiped off my finger and I found myself blushing at how close he was to me. Thankfully he wasn't looking at me.

"Um, Stevens?"

"Yeah?"

"What happens if no one claims me?"

He smiled and said, "I don't think that will happen, but we'll cross that bridge when it comes."

Bridge? What bridge? Why were we going across a bridge? And how would it come to us? Or was he taking me somewhere?

He left and the woman came back a bit later to put something in the weird line in my arm. She asked me how I felt and then left again, leaving me alone in this weird place. I slept for a bit and then the first man came back in and shined a light in my eyes. "Well, you don't have a concussion."

"That's good?"

"Yes."

"So, do I have to stay here until someone claims me?" I asked him.

He rubbed his chin and said, "Well, we want to keep you at least another day for observation. It's very odd that you only remember your age and name, but nothing else."

"I wish I could remember," I told him honestly.

He patted my shoulder and said, "Don't stress yourself over it. If you try too hard, you might end up hurting yourself."

"Okay."

"Are you hungry?"

"Yes."

"I'll have the nurse bring you some food."

"What's a nurse?"

"That's what the lady who is helping you is called. I'm a doctor and she is a nurse."

"Oh, okay. Thank you, Doctor."

He nodded his head and mumbled to himself as he left. The nurse lady came back a bit later with a tray of food and I ate every last piece of the odd foods. She brought me more and I ate most of that as well. The rest of the night, she and Doctor asked me lots of questions to see what I did and didn't know. It was boring and tiring and made me feel frustrated and overwhelmed.

The next morning, Stevens came back with a worried expression. "Well we couldn't find your fingerprints in the database and you don't match any of the missing persons' reports."

"What does that all mean?" I asked.

"It means that you're essentially a Jane Doe, except that you know your first name," he said with a sigh.

"What are you going to do?"

He sat down and looked me in the eyes. "Do you remember anything else about yourself?"

I shook my head. "I've been trying to remember anything, but I can't."

"Well, normally they would just release you from the hospital," he said.

"But I have no place to live," I whispered sadly. I didn't know where to go or where to get food.

Doctor walked in and smiled at us. "Hello, how are you today, Alys?"

"Not good," I whispered, "I don't have a home to go to or food out there. I don't want to live in the mountains."

"Well the good news is that your blood tests came back clean."

"You tested my blood? For what?"

"Yes, we had to make sure that you weren't using drugs."

"What are drugs?"

"Have you ever encountered a case like this before?" Stevens asked Doctor with a serious frown on his face.

He shook his head. "No, I haven't encountered a case myself, but there was a man who didn't remember anything about himself once. Normally people forget things after a certain point and can't retain those memories, not this way. And it's even more odd that she knows her name and age."

"Is it scary outside?" I asked Doctor and Stevens.

"Scary?" Doctor asked, "What do you mean?"

"You know, out there? Are there a lot of animals that could hurt me? Or bad people? Is there somewhere I could find trees with fruits or something to eat?"

"It doesn't exactly work like that here," Stevens said sadly.

"What do you mean?" This was so confusing.

"You can't just take fruit from trees because they probably belong to someone," he explained.

"Someone owns the trees?!" I asked in shock. How could someone own trees?

"I've got to make my rounds," Doctor explained and then left me alone with Stevens.

"You can't remember anything else?" he asked me softly.

"No," I whispered. "I'm trying, but I don't remember anything else."

"I have to leave," he told me.

I didn't want him to leave. I wasn't sure why, but I felt better when he was with me. "Oh, okay. Will I see you again?"

He nodded his head. "Hopefully, I will have good news for you when I see you again."

He opened the door and turned back one last time. "Bye, Alys."

"Bye, Stevens."

He let the door shut and I relaxed on the bed. What had happened to me? What was going to happen to me? I couldn't imagine finding food if people owned the trees. Did they own the animals too? What a strange place!

I slept on and off most of the day with the nurse checking on me periodically and giving me strange things to eat and drink. The sun set and I was incredibly bored. I screamed into my hands and the door to my room opened.

"Are you okay?" Stevens asked me with pinched eyebrows and a frown.

"Oh, hi," I said in shock.

He walked in and I realized he wasn't wearing the same shirt with the gold thing. "Are you in pain?" he asked.

"No, just bored," I admitted.

He smiled and then laughed lightly. "Oh, good. I was worried." He was worried about me? "I thought you might be bored and that you could use some company...Would you like me to keep you company?"

His body was stiff and he hadn't moved away from the door. Why was he nervous? "You want to keep me company?" I asked softly.

"Yeah, I brought some stuff to entertain us," he said, "If you want to, that is."

"That sounds great!" I said with a broad smile.

His shoulders relaxed and he walked to the side of my bed and sat in the chair there. "I wasn't sure what you liked so I brought a few different things." He took the bag off his shoulder and opened it. Inside were brightly colored packages and some cans. He opened one of the packages and handed it to me. I took one of the items out and ate it. It was crunchy and salty.

"That's good," I said and got a smile in return.

He lifted a little piece of the can and it made a strange sound and opened a small oval hole. "Here, try this."

I took the can from him. "Oh, it's cold," I commented in shock. I tilted the can to get the liquid out and swallowed it. "Whoa, sugary."

"Do you remember what that's called?" he asked me. I shook my head. "Soda."

"Soda."

I folded my legs under me to give us more room and he took out several other items and we put the open bags in the middle of the bed on top of the sheets. He sat down on the other end of my bed with the food between us and ate with me. "What's your favorite?" he asked me after I'd sampled everything.

"This and this," I said and pointed at two items.

"Those are chocolate and called M&Ms and those are chips and called Doritos."

"Doritos are really good," I said around another chip.

"You should try Doritos nachos. That is amazing," he told me with a smirk.

The nurse walked in, but stopped when she saw Stevens. "Officer Stevens," she said. "I didn't know you were here."

"Just keeping Alys company," he explained, but his shoulders were tense again and he was frowning.

"That's nice of you," she said and smiled, but she didn't look happy. She checked the machines around me and asked me, "How are you feeling?"

"Fine."

"No headaches?" she asked.

I shook my head.

"Good. Well, have fun," she told us and left the room. As she was closing the door, I saw her shake her head. What was her problem? Why didn't she like Stevens being here?

"Are you tired?" Stevens asked me.

"No. I slept a lot today since there wasn't really anything else to do."

"Do you like to draw?" he asked.

"Draw?"

"Draw or color? I know it's probably childish, but it's something I do occasionally."

"Maybe, I'd like to try."

He pulled out a book and a box and set them between us. He flipped the book open and it was a blank sheet of paper. He opened the box and it was filled with sticks of different colors.

He took one of the colors and made a design on the page with it. "I'm not a great artist, but sometimes it's relaxing and helps time go by," he told me as he continued to draw. When he stopped, I stared in shock at the pretty butterfly.

"That's pretty," I told him. I didn't think I could do something like that. He handed me the stick and I made a couple practice marks on the page and started drawing. I traded colors out and then after I was done I leaned back to look at it.

"What is it?" he asked me as he examined it.

I shrugged. "I don't know. It just felt right to draw it." The design was some type of symbol. I wasn't sure what, though.

"Can I take this with me when I leave tonight?" he asked.

"You want it?" I asked in shock. He nodded his head. "Sure."

He tore the page out, folded the paper and put it in his bag. "Do you want to learn to play tick-tack-toe, if you don't remember?" he asked me.

I nodded my head. "I would like to learn."

He drew some lines on the page and then drew a circle in the center one. "So, I'm o's and your x's. The goal is to get three of your marks in a row, this way, this way, or this way," he explained while showing the directions. "You get to make one mark at a time. So, since I went, now you go."

I put my x in the top right corner and then he drew his next one beside his. I put mine next to mine and then he drew a third circle next to his and drew a line through it.

"I won."

"What?"

"You should have put your x here," he put an x through where his third circle was, "if you had done that you would have blocked me so that I couldn't win."

"Oh, I think I get it now," I told him.

He drew a new set of lines and we went again. We filled the

boxes up and no one got three in a row. "That's called a 'Cat's Game' because no one won."

"Why does the cat get it?" I asked curiously.

He chuckled. "It's just the name. I'm not really sure where it came from."

"Oh...again?" I requested.

I lost track of time and of how many games we played, but Stevens was yawning and my eyelids were growing heavier. "Time for me to head home," he said and stretched his arms up over his head. He was *really* handsome and incredibly nice for doing this for me.

I helped him pack up his bag, but kept the book and the coloring sticks. We stood up and I said, "Thank you for keeping me company and for the food and for the drawing stuff."

He smiled and said, "You're welcome, Alys."

I fidgeted with the ugly weird gown I was wearing and asked, "Could you come tomorrow?"

He nodded his head. "I'll be by tomorrow before they discharge you. Hopefully, someone who knows you will have contacted us by then."

I suddenly felt sad and alone. I looked at the floor and whispered, "I don't think anyone will."

"Don't worry about it," he told me. "We'll figure everything out tomorrow, okay?"

I nodded and watched him leave. At least there was one nice person in this place.

I hardly slept and to keep my boredom at bay, I continued drawing. I wasn't sure what the things I was drawing were, but I felt compelled to draw them. I found another drawing utensil in my room that the nurse or Doctor had left and used that to try to draw. It worked better for drawing faces and as I was finishing a drawing of Stevens he came in.

"What are you drawing?" he asked me with a smile.

I closed the book so he couldn't see the picture, feeling embarrassed that he would catch me drawing him. "Nothing."

"Come on, let me see," he begged.

I slowly held out the book to him. He flipped through the pages and was frowning when he got to my first drawings of men I didn't know and then he froze when he got to the last picture, his.

"It's not good and I'm sorry. I was just drawing whatever came to mind and, well, um, you did." I felt my cheeks grow hot and looked down at my hands so I wouldn't have to see his expression anymore.

"It's really good," he told me.

I looked up at him in shock. "Really?"

He nodded his head while staring at the page. "It is."

"Are you mad?" I asked.

He looked at me with wide eyes. "No. Why would I be mad?"

"I don't know."

"Do you know these other people that you drew?" he asked and showed me the pictures again.

I shook my head. "No." They weren't complete, some of their features missing like their noses or the eyes mostly erased because it didn't feel right, but I just couldn't finish them for some reason.

"Did anyone claim me?" I asked.

He set the book down on the bed and sat on the end of it. "No, but we're still checking into some things. We're spreading your picture around all over in hopes of finding someone."

"What if no one does?" I asked him nervously and felt fear growing in me. "What if I don't know anyone? Will I have to be homeless? Or will I have to live with strangers I don't know?" What if someone tried to hurt me in a new home?

Stevens studied me a moment and then asked, "What would you say if I offered for you to come live with me?"

"Live. With you?" I asked him nervously.

He nodded his head. "I hate the idea of you living on the streets. A pretty girl like you could get into a lot of trouble out there."

"I don't want to be a burden," I whispered as I looked down at my clasped hands. He had called me pretty!

"I live alone and I work a lot, but I have an extra bedroom with a bed and cable and you could stay with me until we figure out where you're from."

"Really?" I asked him as tears fell down my face.

He smiled at me and said, "Really."

"You're very nice."

He laughed nervously. "Thank you. I'm going to talk to the doctor about you getting discharged."

I nodded even though I didn't know what discharged meant, and watched him leave. Was everyone as nice as him? No, because Doctor and the nurse didn't offer for me to live with them.

What if he was a bad guy? I shook my head. He didn't seem like a bad guy. Surely if he was so important and Doctor and the nurse deferred to him then he couldn't be bad. And what bad guy would bring a stranger snacks and drawing things? I sat alone for a bit longer and then the nurse came in with a couple more women in the same outfits. "Hi," I greeted them since that was what you were supposed to do when someone came to see you. I wasn't sure how I knew that, but I knew that was right.

"We brought you some extra clothes we had, since the ones you were wearing were ruined and you don't have any others," the nurse said as she and the women all smiled at me.

I looked at the weird colored clothes in her hands and forced a smile. "Thank you."

She set the clothes on the chair beside my bed and said, "We weren't sure your bra size so we don't have that for you, but you don't really need a bra with how you're built."

"What's a bra?" I asked as I held up a shirt with a large animal's face with its mouth open on it.

"It holds up your..." one of the women said and then put her hands under her breasts and made them move up and down.

"Oh." *Why would you need them held up?* I wondered.

"You better be good to Stevens," one of the women said bitterly, "he's a great guy and he doesn't need someone hurting him."

"I wouldn't hurt anybody," I said in shock.

"Nancy, that's enough," the nurse snapped at the woman who had spoken.

Nancy looked down at her feet and red blossomed on her cheeks.

"Well, we will let you get dressed," the nurse said.

"Thank you for this generosity," I said to them with a bright smile.

"You're welcome, dear."

As soon as they left I took off the stupid gown I had been wearing since I woke up. The dumb thing wasn't even sewn together all the way and had to be tied to stay together. I set it on the bed and then examined all of the clothes before putting them on in what I hoped to be the right order judging by the clothes the others had worn.

Someone knocked on the door. "Come in," I called as I examined the last piece of clothing I had that I couldn't figure out what to do with.

"The doctor said...Oh, uh, did you need a moment?" Stevens asked with a blush on his face.

"No, I just don't know what this is for," I murmured as I

examined the piece of clothing that had two oval openings of one size and then a third oval of a larger size.

"Those are called underwear," he informed me.

I glanced over at him and asked, "Where does it go? Are you supposed to wear it? I don't see you with it?"

He laughed and said, "They go on under your pants."

Under the pants? Why would you wear something under your pants? Why wear pants if you wore the underwear? "Odd," I whispered.

"I'll just step out so you can put them on," he said as he turned around.

"No, I don't want to wear them," I informed him.

He stopped with a perfectly stunned expression on his face. "Alys, you really should put them on. It's considered weird not to wear them."

"Why do you wear pants if you have these under them?" I asked in frustration.

"It's just what our culture does." He said as he rubbed the back of his neck nervously.

I sighed. "Fine." He walked out and I took off the pants, put the underwear on, and then put the pants back on. "Okay, you can come in."

He came back in and smiled. "Alright, are you ready to leave?"

I nodded vigorously. "Yes, please!"

"I spoke to my Chief and he gave me the rest of the day off so that I could take you to my house and show you everything."

Chief? "Are you in an army?" I asked him as we walked out of the room into a hallway with lots of people walking around in the outfits like the nurse and Doctor.

"No, I'm a police officer," he said.

"What's that?"

"I protect people and arrest bad guys and take them to jail," he said and pushed open a door for me to walk through.

"What's jail?" I asked and stepped out into sunlight. I stopped as soon as I was outside and stared at the world before me.

The ground was made of a weird stone and there were, um, I knew the word...cars! There were cars everywhere! There was also so much noise that my ears hurt. I clamped my hands over my ears and asked, "How can you stand the noise?!"

He smiled sweetly and pulled my hands down. "You'll get used to it soon."

"How long will it take to walk to your house?" I asked him. He walked down stairs towards a black vehicle.

"We're not walking. We're going to drive."

I stared at the car nervously. "In *that*?!"

"Don't worry, it's safe." He pulled open a piece of the car and waved at me to come over. I climbed into it and sat on an oddly-shaped chair. Stevens walked around, opened another section, and sat down. "Okay, shut your door." I looked at the piece that was hanging open, grabbed it and pulled it towards me. It slammed closed with an odd metal click. "Put your seat-belt on."

"What's a seatbelt?" I asked as I looked around the strange vehicle.

He leaned across me and grabbed something above my shoulder. I held my breath as his face was inches from mine. "You have to put one of these on every time you get in a car to keep you safe, okay?" I nodded my head.

He sat back in his chair and put his belt on. I watched in amazement as he put a metal piece into the car and turned it, which made the car start grumbling. Had he angered it?! Was it going to attack us? He didn't seem nervous. Maybe he had a truce with it and it just grumbled when he used it? I held perfectly still as the car began moving and assumed that despite its growling the car probably wasn't going to attack me. I looked at all of the buildings around me that had weird markings all over them. What did they all mean? He drove for a little bit and then he turned towards a building, drove alongside it and started talking to a weird square that had things like the photo of me on it, but of food. "Are you hungry?" he asked. I nodded my head. "What would you like?" I shrugged. "I'll just order for you, okay?" I nodded my head. "I'll take four cheeseburgers, two large fries, and two chocolate milkshakes," he said.

A weird voice spoke back to him from the square thing and then he moved forward. He gave the person in the building some pieces of paper and then he drove to the next opening where that person gave him bags with the food in them. Stevens handed the bags to me and I put them on my lap in silent shock.

"Alys, you alright?" he asked.

"I've never seen anything like that," I whispered, "You gave them paper for food."

He laughed. "It's called money. You use money to buy things, like food."

"Strange," I whispered and opened one of the bags to peek inside. For some reason, I recalled eating a burger before, but I couldn't remember where. "I think I've eaten a burger before," I told him softly.

"Burgers are pretty much a main staple here," he said with a laugh. "We'll eat them as soon as we get to my house."

I closed the bag again and sat patiently, watching the passing scenery in all of its weird glory. What were all of the people walking around doing? Where were they going? Everyone seemed to move so fast, like they were in a hurry.

Stevens stopped in front of a house that was very pretty and was painted a soothing color like the sky. Blue! It was called blue. He removed the metal thing from the car and it stopped grumbling and then he got out, shutting the door behind him. I tried to get the seatbelt off, but it wouldn't let go. "Seatbelt, let go," I ordered it. Nothing happened. Stevens opened my door and I said, "The seatbelt won't let me go."

He smiled, took the bags of food from me, and told me how to make it release me. Once free, I followed him up to the front door while holding cold soft mugs filled with what he had called "chocolate shakes." He used another metal piece to make the door open and stepped into the house, waiting for me to follow. I entered the room and stared at all of the strange devices in it. What did they all do?

He pointed to the closest thing and said, "That's the couch. You can sit on it and watch the TV." He pointed at a large rectangle hanging on the wall. "I'll teach you about the TV later. Under the TV is my gaming console, which I play video games on. Through that door is the kitchen, where we store and make food." He walked up the stairs and pointed to one door on the right. "That's my room." He pointed to the door in the center and said, "That's the bathroom where you can go pee and stuff." He pointed to the door on the left. "And that will be your room." He pushed open the door to my room and waved me forward. I walked into the room and found a bed, a table with a mirror, and some type of tall rectangle with drawers. "That's to put your clothes in," he explained when he saw me staring at it.

"That's a lot of space for clothes," I whispered in shock.

"Oh, I guess you don't really have any clothes. We'll have to buy you some," he said as he rubbed the back of his neck.

This was so much to take in and yet the names were sticking well in my head and I almost seemed to remember some bits about each item after he told me about them.

"Well, let's go downstairs and eat and I will show you how the TV works," he said happily. I followed him down the stairs and we sat down on the couch. He put the bags of food on the table and then divided the food on two plates and pushed one plate towards me.

I took a bite of the burger and said, "This is really good."

He smiled, pleased and said, "I'm glad you like it."

We ate in silence for a bit and then he grabbed what he called a "remote" and turned the TV on. He pushed some buttons and then images flashed across the screen and people were talking to each other and running around.

"What is this?" I asked as I walked towards the TV, reaching for it to touch the people.

"It's called a movie. We record people talking and moving and can even add in special effects that aren't really happening."

A guy's hand was cut off with a sword and blood sprayed all around. "I don't think blood sprays like that when your hand gets cut off," I whispered, shocked that I would know something like that.

"No, it's just a special effect. And his hand isn't really cut off. That's a fake hand."

So odd.

He pressed a button on the remote and then another "movie" came on that was even stranger looking. "This is a cartoon. People draw them and add color and record their voices for the characters' voices."

"Wow," I whispered and sat down beside him again to watch the TV and eat more.

"Try your chocolate shake," he insisted.

I obliged and sputtered at the amount of sugar in it. "That's a lot of sweet."

He laughed. "Yeah, it's usually called a dessert, but most people just drink them nowadays."

"So, tomorrow you're going back to work? What is that?"

"Work is where you go do something and get paid money for

it. I spend my time patrolling and acting as a police officer like I told you."

"And you do that to get money to spend on food?" I asked him.

He nodded his head. "And to pay for this house."

"You have to pay for your house?!" That seemed very odd to me. For some reason, I assumed you were just given a house.

"Yes."

"So, I should get a job to pay for my food and stuff?" I asked him.

"You can't get a job."

"Why not?" I was perfectly capable of doing almost anything.

"Because you don't have identification. You have to know your name and Social Security number to work."

"Oh."

"You don't have to worry about money for now. We'll figure all of this out later. Would you like to go buy some clothes after you're done eating?" he asked me.

"Okay."

"Let me go change clothes real quick," he said and stood up. "Just stay here, okay?"

I nodded my head and watched him walk up the stairs. This was so unusual. I didn't remember much, but I didn't think that people paid for houses where I came from. Where did I come from? Would I ever remember? I ate the rest of my food and grabbed the controller to try to go to a different movie. I pushed a button, but it made the screen change to a loud angry black and white vibrating movie. I yelled in surprise and covered my ears while closing my eyes.

The ground vibrated and then the noise stopped. I opened my eyes to find Stevens standing with the remote in his hand. He had changed into another set of weird clothes, but at least they were more normal looking than his other set. He had on a pair of blue pants and a shirt that matched the color of his eyes, turquoise. I was excited that I could remember the names of the items and colors, but I didn't say anything out loud to him. Now that I saw him closer, he was very handsome. "You okay?" he asked me.

I nodded my head. "I tried to use it, but it got mad, I guess."

He smirked. "You just pushed the wrong button. Here, you see this one and this one that look like arrows? Those are the ones that you push to change the channel. If you want to play video games you click this button." He clicked the button and the screen changed to one with odd symbols all over it.

"What do the symbols mean?" I asked softly.

His eyes widened in disbelief. "You can't read?"

"Read? No. I don't think I can read."

He grimaced. "I'm not a very good teacher. I might be able to find you a class to go to, though."

"Will they teach me to read at the class?" I asked hopefully.

"Yes."

"I would like that."

"Well, let's go get you some clothes, okay?"

I nodded my head and stood up from the couch. "What's that on your back?" I asked him softly. It looked like a weird lump.

He turned his head to look behind him and then met my eyes. "You noticed it?"

I shrugged and felt embarrassed. Was I not supposed to notice it? Was it some type of disfigure that he had and I hadn't noticed before?

"It's my gun," he explained. "Even when I'm off-duty I keep it with me."

"What's a gun?" I asked him as he lifted his shirt to show me the strange metal device.

"It's a weapon."

"Why not carry a sword?" I asked. It made more sense to carry a sword that was capable of cutting off limbs than a hard piece of metal to hit people with.

"A gun shoots a piece of metal very fast and can kill someone from very far away from you," he explained.

Oh, that was definitely better than a sword. "Are you afraid someone might try to kill you?" I asked. Part of me knew that those who protected the innocent were in danger of the bad ones who wanted to do evil things.

"No, but it's better to be prepared." He put his shirt down and opened the door for me. We got into a different car this time and he drove us to what I recalled being called a "mall."

"Stevens, what is life like here?" I asked him as I watched the people hurrying around.

"It's pretty fast-paced with people going to work, out to eat, to the movies, and going home. What your life is like depends on a lot of different factors. For example, my life is much different than the life of a stay-at-home mom."

"What's a stay-at-home mom?" I asked him.

"That's a woman who doesn't work and instead she stays home with her children to raise them."

"How does she earn money for the house?" I asked. I thought everyone had to work.

"Usually the husband works to pay for the house in that situation."

"Do you have a wife?" I asked him.

He blushed and said, "No, I don't. I am what is called 'single,' which means that I don't have a wife or girlfriend."

"Is that a bad thing?" I asked softly.

"Not necessarily. Some people think you should be married with kids by my age though."

"How old are you?"

"Twenty-four."

"Why don't you have a girlfriend?"

He sighed. "Well, I had a girlfriend for a while, but due to my work schedule at the time I didn't spend much time with her and she decided that she needed someone that could be there more for her."

"Oh, well her loss."

He smiled. "I agree."

"Do you have parents?" I asked softly. If I had them, I couldn't remember them. Maybe they were dead.

"My mom died a few years ago," he explained, "and I've never known my dad."

"I'm sorry. I wish I could remember my parents."

"Hopefully in time, you'll start remembering," he said with a warm smile.

He stopped the car and unbuckled his seat belt. I looked down at mine and pushed the red button like he had shown me and it released me. "You're remembering everything I'm teaching you, which is a good sign."

We got out of the car and I followed him into a building that roared with noise. I grimaced at the loudness and stayed close to Stevens' side. He noticed my discomfort and smiled encouragingly.

"It's loud," I explained.

"Your ears should adjust soon," he said.

There were so many people in this building! They moved around from one opening to another, talking with people near them as they walked, but it didn't seem like they talked to anyone who went by, only the people they were with.

"Do you know these people?" I asked him.

He shook his head. "No, there are too many people in this city for me to know each of them."

"So, you just walk by each other and never meet?" It seemed so odd to me.

"The majority of the time, yeah." He veered towards stairs that moved on their own up towards a higher area. I stared at the odd device in fear. What if it tried to eat me? He took my hand and gently tugged. "It's alright, just put one foot on and then the other. The stairs just move us up without having to walk ourselves." I knew I was gripping his hand too hard, but I couldn't make myself relax as I stepped on one stair as it came out of the floor and then the next. I yelped in surprise as we were propelled upwards, although not as fast as I thought it would go. "See, easy."

"Strange," I whispered.

"You'll have to step off at the top."

I followed his lead and took several steps away from it. Children hopped on and off of the device happily. I felt like a fool to see children doing it so easily when I had been so frightened.

He tugged on my hand, which I realized he was still holding, and said, "The store's right over here."

Without mentioning our joined hands, I followed him into a room with rows and rows of clothes. He walked up to a pretty woman and she smiled warmly at him. "Detective Stevens," she said happily. "I haven't seen you in a couple years. How are you?"

"Good, Gabriella," he said with a smile for her.

I felt jealousy in my chest and pushed it down. I had no reason to be jealous.

"And who are you?" she asked me.

"Alys," I whispered as I looked out over all of the clothes. Did she own all of these clothes?

"Oh, you're the Jane Doe case!" she said excitedly.

"What? I'm Alys, not Jane," I explained. Was *she* damaged in the head?

She smiled sweetly at me and nodded. "Right. So, what can I do for you?"

"Can you help her find some clothes? She doesn't have any and she's going to need some until we can find a family or relative of hers," Stevens said and let go of my hand.

"Of course! Do you know what size you are?" she asked me.

"Size?"

"We'll just guess and figure it out as we go," she said instead of explaining. "Stevens, why don't you go sit in the red chairs over there." She pointed to some vibrant, red chairs on the far side of the room and then walked away from us to the first row of clothes.

"She'll help you out. I'll just sit over there, okay? I won't leave the store," he told me with a serious expression.

I rubbed my arm nervously, but nodded my head in understanding. I didn't like the idea of being alone with this girl, but if he was still here I felt better.

"Do you have a color preference?" she asked me as she took several items from the rows and dangled them over her arm.

"Uh, not really."

"What about style? Do you prefer dresses or pants?"

"Both?" I really wasn't sure what she was talking about, but I figured that since she owned so many clothes she would know what I should wear.

The amount of clothes on her arm grew and grew until she finally said, "This is a good start," and walked towards an area in front of where Stevens was sitting that had small rooms. She opened the door and motioned for me to enter. I followed her in and she shut the door behind me. "Now, I know they said you don't remember much, so do you remember how to put on clothes?"

"Um, a little bit, but some of your clothes are strange," I admitted. I almost told her about not liking the underwear, but

Stevens had seemed adamant about the fact that I needed to wear them. "The nurse didn't have a bra for me, but she said she wasn't sure I needed one. I'm not sure what a bra even is."

"Girls of your size don't really need one, but it's still a good idea to wear one so they don't start drooping," she said and pulled out a long piece of cloth with markings on it.

"What's that?"

"It's a measuring tape. I'm going to measure you to figure out what size bra you need."

"What is one?" I asked.

"It's this," she lifted her shirt to show me a small piece of clothing around her breasts that her huge ones practically bulged out of.

"Oh." Another garment under one you were already wearing. "So you wear a bra and shirt?" I asked her.

She nodded her head. "You wear underwear and a bra all the time, except when showering and some girls don't wear them when sleeping."

Things were so odd here. "Okay."

She made me lift my arms so she could measure me and then instructed me to start trying on the pants that she had hung up on the left side of the small room while she went to find a bra. I put on one and it was too big. I put on another and it fit, but it dug into my skin. I found a third that fit, but the part around my legs was too tight for my comfort. After a few more I finally found one I liked. She came back with a few different bras and smiled at the pants. "Those look good on you."

"Thanks," I mumbled as I looked at myself in the mirror. They did make my butt look good.

"Let's try this bra on," she said. "Take off your shirt."

I felt a little uncomfortable undressing in front of her, but Stevens had told me she would help me. She showed me how to put on the bra, which was more like a weird torture device to squeeze my breasts against my chest. She put a different one on and that one wasn't as tight. Then she had me try on one of the shirts and pushed me outside in front of Stevens.

"That looks nice," he said with a smile.

I blushed and played with the end of the shirt.

"Okay, one outfit down."

I lost track of how many pieces of clothing I put on and showed to Stevens. My stomach grew hungry and as I tried on the last item, a soft pink dress, I could hear it grumbling. I stepped outside to show Stevens and his eyes widened.

"You don't like this one?" I guessed. I thought I looked cute in it, but this style was different than I thought it should be.

"You look beautiful," he whispered.

"That's because she is beautiful," Gabriella said. "Alright! We're done. Do you want to wear that one the rest of the day?"

"No, I want to wear the first outfit." I wasn't sure I could handle Stevens looking at me like he was all day. I turned around without looking at Stevens again and changed into the other outfit. She grabbed all of the clothes and carried them up to the front where we had first seen her.

Stevens took out the thing that held his paper money and took out a strange plastic rectangle. "What's that?" I asked curiously.

"That's a credit card," he explained.

"What's it do?"

"It is connected to the bank where all of my money is and lets me use it without carrying all that money around in my pocket."

"Whoa."

"It is pretty cool," he agreed.

Gabriella folded up the clothes and put them in bags and I watched as he slid the card in a device and then pushed buttons on it a few times.

"Thanks for coming," she said with a wide smile.

"Thanks for your help," Stevens thanked her.

"Thank you," I said to her.

"If you need anything else, call me. I'm more than willing to help."

"Thanks," Stevens said and grabbed the bags.

"I should carry those," I told him and reached for them.

"You can carry a few," he told me.

Why did he want to carry them? Was it because he had used the money from his work?

"Did it cost a lot?" I asked him softly. There were a lot of clothes.

"Don't worry about it," he told me adamantly.

"I wish I could work to pay you back," I said with a sigh.

He laughed. "I appreciate the thought, but it's okay."

"Where are we going now?" I asked.

He looked down at the sandals I was wearing and said, "We need to get you a pair of shoes."

"What's wrong with my sandals? They're comfortable." They were very comfortable. I felt like I had had them my entire life.

"They're not ideal for running in," he said.

"I can run perfectly fine in them," I argued.

"Well, let's just get you a pair for my sake, okay?"

"Okay." He was pretty stubborn.

He stepped into a store that had shoes all over the walls. There were so many different shapes and colors and they looked so strange. "Go ahead and take off your sandals," Stevens said and set the bags he had been carrying on the ground next to a bench.

I sat down on the bench and untied my sandals. Part of me felt like I was taking a piece of myself off, but I did it because Stevens asked me to. I set my sandals on the bench and Stevens brought over a weird metal thing and slid one of my feet onto it. I jerked my foot back from the coldness and he laughed softly. "I know, it's cold, but if you could just put your foot back on it and stand up, I'll figure out your size and you can start trying on shoes."

I did as he asked and he adjusted my foot on it before deciding on something and pulling it out from under my foot. I sat down as he began taking boxes from stacks that were all around the room and carried three over to me. He handed me two brown fuzzy balls and said, "Put those on your feet."

I looked at the balls and back up at him. "How?"

He laughed and said, "You take things for granted when you're used to them. Like this." He pulled the balls out and then slipped my foot inside one of the things. It stretched until it covered my entire foot.

"There are so many weird things," I whispered.

He put the other one on and then opened a box and put one of the shoes on my foot. It felt restrictive and warm. He put a second shoe on my left foot and said, "Walk around in them a bit and let me know what you think."

I walked around the store and was surprised at how comfortable they were. I couldn't feel the ground and as odd as it was, the shoes were soft on the bottoms of my feet. I squatted down and then jumped up and landed on my feet. "Wow, they're really soft."

"Does your heel slip in them or do your toes feel squished?"

I shook my head and walked back over to him. He pushed on the end of my big toe and said, "They seem to fit pretty well. Do you like them?" I nodded my head. As much as I felt like I couldn't let the sandals go, these shoes were way more comfortable. "Can I keep my sandals?" I asked.

He smiled and nodded his head. "Of course."

He put the other boxes away and went up to give a man the

empty box for the shoes I was wearing and gave him the credit card.

I put my sandals inside one of the bags and then picked up a bunch of the bags before he got back. I stood with a smile on my face when he was done. He smiled back and picked up the rest of the bags. "Are you hungry?"

I nodded my head and followed him again. "How big is this building?"

"It's pretty big, but not the biggest mall. The biggest one is about an hour from here."

"Why do you need a bigger one?"

"It has more stores and more options for buying items."

"Who needs so much stuff?" I asked him in shock.

He laughed. "That's a question people have been asking for a long time."

The smell of food drifted to me and soon I could see a big area with lots of people and images of food on the walls. "What is this?"

"This is a food court. It's where you can choose from a few different places to eat."

"They all sell different foods?" I asked in shock.

"Yeah, that one sells pizza, that one sells burgers, that one sells Chinese food..."

He listed off several other types that I had no idea what they meant and then headed towards the sitting area. He set the bags underneath a table and said, "Why don't you sit here and save our seat while I get food for us?"

"Okay."

I sat down in the uncomfortable chair and watched the people around me. There were so many different looking people and all of many different ages. I looked at the different groups of people and wondered if I would ever be able to fit in here. I felt like I didn't belong here and yet I had to, right? What had happened to make me lose my memory?

"Hi," a man said from across my table. I didn't recognize him.

"Hello."

"Are you alone?"

"Right now, but..."

He sat down before I could finish my sentence. "I'm Jason," he said, extending his hand out to me.

"Alys," I said as I stared at his hand. What was I supposed to do with it?

He pulled his hand back and the smile slipped off his face. "Not a hand shaker? It's cool. So, what's a beautiful woman like you do here alone?"

"She's not alone," Stevens said from behind Jason with a tray of food in his hand.

"Oh, hey Stevens."

"Markston. What are you doing here?" Stevens asked as he set the food tray down and folded his arms across his chest. He looked angry. Had I done something wrong? Was I not supposed to talk to this guy?

"Today's my day off, so I thought I would come hang out at the mall," Jason or Markston or whatever his name actually was, said. "I didn't know you had a girlfriend," he said with a smirk as he looked at me. He looked at me a bit longer and then his eyes widened. "I thought I recognized your face! You're the Jane Doe! Oh, ho, ho, Stevens, you better hope that there isn't a husband or boyfriend to come and claim her. I always knew you were a sly dog."

"It's not like that, Markston, but you'll think whatever you want anyways," Stevens said and sat down beside me.

"What's this?" I asked as I inspected the food.

"This is called pizza," Stevens said.

Steam was rising from it so I knew it was hot, but he didn't bring any utensils. "How do you eat it?"

"Wow, she really doesn't remember anything, does she?" Markston...Jason asked.

"I'm Alys and I'm eighteen," I told him angrily. "And I don't think I like you."

Stevens laughed and Markston just smiled. "She's a good judge of character at least," Stevens said.

"Yeah, yeah, laugh it up while you can, Stevens. I'll see you later. It was nice to meet you, Alys."

"Bye," I said as I watched Stevens pick up the pizza and eat it while holding it in his hands.

I copied him and took a bite and chewed. It was chewy, cheesy and really good.

"Do you like it?" he asked.

I nodded my head and took another bite. "Yes."

"Good," he said happily.

We ate in silence a bit and then I asked, "Stevens? Was I not supposed to talk to him?"

"Who? Markston?"

I nodded my head.

He set his pizza down and sighed. "We tell children not to talk to strangers, but that's because they could lie to them and steal them away. I don't think you would fall for that, but it's still better to be safe than sorry."

"You don't like him, do you?"

He shrugged. "He's an alright guy. I just know he likes to play the field."

"Huh?" What did that mean?

He rubbed the back of his neck, his sign that he was uncomfortable. "He sleeps with a lot of different women."

I think he was referring to the other thing, not sleeping, but

I didn't ask him to clarify. "I wouldn't do that with him anyway," I mumbled as I played with my plate.

"Oh? He's not your type, huh?"

"He's got some crazy in his eyes that I don't like." Stevens laughed and I felt stupid. "That's not something people normally say, is it?"

"Some people say that, but it's just surprising to hear you say it."

"Sorry," I mumbled.

"You don't need to apologize. You didn't say anything wrong."

"Do you think I'll learn to fit back in here?" I asked him.

"I think you're already doing a great job."

A group of people started yelling loudly and Stevens turned towards it. "Maybe we should go," I suggested.

Two very loud bangs sounded from where the arguing was going on and people instantly started screaming in fear. Stevens had his gun in his hand, our table turned on its side, and had pulled me behind it before I knew what was happening. People started running away from the food court in all different directions with fear on their faces. I felt afraid even though I wasn't sure what the sound had been and wanted to yell someone's name for help, but the name wouldn't come. My head started hurting and I clutched it tightly. Why did I want to yell someone's name when I was afraid? Who was it? Was there someone who usually protected me?

Stevens peeked over the top of the table and said, "I want you to stay here, okay?"

I nodded my head and he moved from behind our table. "Put the weapon down," Markston shouted.

"Nice and easy, boys," Stevens said.

Some other guys started yelling and then there were more bangs. I clenched my teeth as I fought to yell and wished I could at least remember who I wanted to yell for and why! Did I have a boyfriend or someone who protected me?

There was a silence that scared me even more than the bangs. I leaned out just enough to see around the table and exhaled in relief when I saw Stevens walking forward. At least he was okay. He talked with someone and so did Markston and then a few minutes later Stevens squatted down in front of me.

"Are you okay?" he asked me.

I nodded my head. "You?"

"Yeah, I'm fine." He looked sad and relief overwhelmed me. I wrapped my arms around his neck in a hug and he hugged me back. "It's going to be a little while before we leave. They're sending some guys over and I'll have to give a statement. They'll probably want a statement from you too."

I nodded my head, but didn't let go. He hugged me a bit longer and then stood up. "What's a statement?"

"You tell them what you saw and heard," he explained, set the table back up right and moved the chairs back. "You can sit here if you want."

"Can I stay with you?" I asked him in a whisper.

He smiled and nodded his head. Without asking, I grabbed his hand and stayed right next to his side as he walked towards the other side of the food court. There was a man sitting with his hands behind his back and another man lying on the ground, both with Markston watching them closely.

I stared at the man lying on the ground and realized. "He's dead, isn't he?"

Stevens nodded his head. "He aimed his gun at Markston to shoot him."

"Did he shoot him?" I asked in shock.

He shook his head. "No, we shot him first."

"Good."

He looked at me in shock. "Good?"

I nodded my head. "Bad people shouldn't be allowed to kill good people."

"It's never good to kill anyone."

"If it's the bad people or the good people, then you always choose the good people to live," I said. I wasn't sure why I was so adamant about this, but I was. "I don't think you should feel bad about saving Markston's life."

"I don't feel bad about saving him, but I do feel bad about killing that guy."

"Why?"

"Because he is dead. He won't be able to do anything else with his life."

"He's the one who shot the first shots, right?"

"Yes, he shot the other man who is sitting there."

"So, you saved Markston and probably that man from getting shot again. You saved two people by killing one bad person. If he had lived, he could have killed more people. He could have killed you or me."

Stevens' jaw clenched. "I'm glad you weren't sitting closer to him."

"Me too."

Several men in outfits like Stevens had worn earlier came towards us. Some went to Markston and the men and some came towards us.

"Stevens," one of the men greeted while the rest stared at me curiously. I resisted the urge to hide behind him. The man smiled at me. "Hello, Alys."

"Hi," I whispered and gripped Stevens' hand harder. He rubbed his thumb across my hand.

"We need to get your statements," the man said.

Stevens nodded his head and started to walk away with the man, but I wouldn't let go of his hand. The other three men were still just staring at me. He looked at the men and said,

"Don't harass her while I'm gone." They nodded their heads. "Alys, you need to stay over here. We have to give our statements separately."

"I don't want to stay here," I whispered as softly as I could.

"They're not going to hurt you. They're just curious about you."

"They're staring at me."

"Well, you are very interesting."

I didn't want to. I didn't want to stay here with these strange men while he went away. He pulled his hand out of mine and smiled reassuringly at me before walking away. I wrapped my arms around myself, digging my hand into my armpit and stared at the ground.

"Would you like to sit down?" one of the men asked me.

I nodded my head without looking at them. There was a loud scraping sound and then a chair in front of me. I sat in it and continued to stare at the ground. I could feel their gazes on me. It was peculiar.

"Can you believe that the one afternoon he takes off, he runs into some crap like this?" one of them asked.

"He always seems to run into trouble when he takes time off," another said.

"You think she really doesn't remember anything or is she just lying because she is running from something or someone?" the third one asked.

I looked up and glared at the three of them since I didn't know who had said what. "If I was making it up, I wouldn't stay at a cop's house," I snapped. "Or your systems should have found me with those fingerprint things and photo."

"You can't just have appeared out of thin air," the middle one said with an attitude. "Everyone has to get a birth certificate and social. You're way too old to have bypassed all systems."

"Maybe she is an alien," the one on the right said with a laugh.

"No, the hospital would have noticed when they tested her blood," the left one said.

"I'm not an alien." I didn't think. What was an alien?

"She speaks pretty good English," the one on the right said.

"I'm a fast learner," I whispered and turned away from them.

"Or just a good liar."

"I thought I told you not to harass her," Stevens said angrily as he walked towards me.

"We were just talking to her," the rude one said.

"I'm not lying," I snapped at him and stood up out of the chair.

"Alys, I need to get your statement now. Can you follow me?" the man who had greeted us initially asked.

I followed him silently and heard Stevens speaking angrily to the three men. Jerks. The man sat down and I sat across from him.

"Alright, why don't you tell me what happened?" he asked as he pushed the button on a device and started writing on a piece of paper.

"What's that?" I asked and pointed at the device.

"It's a recorder; it will record what we say so I can play it back later if I need to."

Did the strange devices have no end? I told him what I remembered happening and then he walked me back to Stevens. "All done?" Stevens asked.

"Yeah, you guys can head on out," the man said.

"She's staying with me if you need any follow-up questions," Stevens told him.

The man handed me a square piece of paper. "If you remember anything, you can call me at this number."

I looked at the paper with markings on it. "Why is he giving me money?" I asked Stevens softly.

Two of the other men laughed and Stevens said, "That's his business card. It has his name and ways to contact him on it."

I handed it to Stevens and said, "I don't understand how those symbols translate to instructions on contacting him."

"You've got to be kidding me. She can't read?" the middle jerk said.

"No, I can't," I said and blushed.

"Maybe someone hid her out in the sticks and only taught her to speak," one of the men said.

"That's possible, but how did she get here? She would have had to travel pretty far," the other man said.

"Come on, let's get your stuff and go home," Stevens said.

I followed him and picked up some of the bags while he picked up the others. We walked by a group of cops and they stared at me openly. "Why does everyone have to stare? Will they stop staring eventually?" I asked.

"I think men will always stare at you."

"Why?" I asked.

"Well, um, because you're pretty."

"Why does that mean they're going to stare at me?" I asked in confusion.

"Men like to look at pretty women."

"That's dumb," I whispered. "Why not talk to the woman instead of staring at her?"

He laughed. "You act like it's so easy. It's not that easy to approach a woman."

"So, if you hadn't met me at the hospital and just saw me on the street, would you talk to me?"

He exhaled loudly. "I know I would definitely want to, but I'm not sure if I would be confident enough to actually do it."

"That's silly. You're very confident. You went right into action when the bangs happened."

"Gunshots," he said.

"What?"

"The bangs were gunshots. He shot the gun he had."

"Oh."

"And yes, but I've been trained to do that."

"You're not trained to talk to women?"

"You spend most of your life trying to figure that all out, but it's still hard most of the time."

"Well then, I would have had to talk to you first if you wouldn't talk to me," I told him adamantly.

He smiled at me and said, "Is that so?"

I nodded my head. "Yes."

"If a man doesn't have the courage to even speak to you then you shouldn't give him your attention," a man said behind us.

I turned around and stared at the man. He looked...familiar. "Do I know you?" I asked him softly.

"Come on, Alys," Stevens said.

I stared at the man and his piercing silver eyes and I felt drawn to them, but I broke free and obeyed Stevens, walking towards the car.

"I'll see you soon, Alys," the man said.

I wasn't sure what he meant, but Stevens turned and said, "You stay away from her."

The man smiled and asked, "You think you could stop me, mortal?"

Mortal? What was he talking about?

"I mean it. Stay away from her."

Stevens pushed me forward and we walked faster towards the car, but I couldn't help glancing back one last time at the man with silver eyes. When I looked at him he looked sad. Who was he? Was he just some crazy guy? Or did he know me?

We got into the car and I asked, "What if he knows me?"

"He doesn't," Stevens said adamantly, "That guy is just a nut job."

"But what if..."

"If he does know you, he will go down to the police station and tell them. Then they'll research his claim. We're not going to let some random guy come and take you if we don't have proof that he knows you. Everyone knows your name, so just because he said it doesn't mean anything. He could be a murderer or rapist who thinks you're an easy target because you're an unknown person right now. If he took you, he could kill you."

I didn't think that man would kill me. I wasn't sure why I thought that, but I was pretty certain. "I understand," I told him. Because I did. I understood that some crazy people could claim to know me and then just hurt me.

We didn't talk the entire drive back to his house or when we climbed up the stairs and put all the clothes in my room.

"Stevens," I whispered.

"Hm?" he asked as he began helping me take the tags off of the clothes.

"I'm sorry. I know you can't just let me go with someone who acts like they know me. I didn't mean to make you upset. And I'm sorry that because of me you had to kill that man..."

"You didn't make me kill him," he said in shock, putting the shirt down he had been holding.

"If you hadn't taken me to get clothes, you wouldn't have been there." I was crying because I felt sad for almost getting him killed. I was crying because I felt so lost and so confused.

He stood up and hugged me. "It's not your fault at all. If I hadn't been there, Markston might have been shot and who knows who else. You didn't have anything to do with that guy's actions."

"I swear I'm not lying," I told him and tried to put as much of my honesty into that statement as I could so he would know.

"I know, Alys. Those guys are just idiots. I know you're not lying about not knowing who you were before or where you're from." He rubbed my back and it began to calm me.

I realized that his gun wasn't on his back where I was hugging him. "Where's your gun?" I asked him and wiped at my eyes.

"They took it for testing and evidence."

"But now you don't have a gun..."

He put a finger on my lips and said, "It's fine. I don't need it until I go back to work." His finger was warm against my lips. He pulled it back and stared at me in shock. "Why don't we finish putting your clothes away?" he asked in a deep voice.

Why had his voice changed? I nodded my head and went back to taking the tags off like he had shown me. We worked in silence and soon finished taking the tags off. Then he showed me how to fold them and put them in the drawers.

"Tomorrow I will show you how to use the washing machine," he told me.

"Aren't you working tomorrow?"

"No, I have some time off the next week or so," he said with a smile.

"Oh, okay," I said happily. I was glad that he would be here to teach me things.

"Want to watch a movie?" he asked. I nodded. He started picking up the tags that hadn't made it into the bag and I bent down to help, but that put my face really close to his.

We looked up at the same time and were so close that our breaths mingled together. He looked at my lips and then up at my face and then stood up quickly and walked out of the room. "I'll go pick out a movie."

I put my fingers against my lips and sat on the bed. I had

wanted to kiss him, but I hadn't done it. What if he didn't like me like that? He was helping me, but that was just because he was nice. And even if he did think I was beautiful he said he didn't think he could have come to talk to me if we hadn't met already. Had I kissed someone before? Was there another man I had kissed?

I changed into the clothes Gabriella had called pajamas and walked down the stairs to sit on the couch.

"I'm making popcorn," he informed me and then something started making a weird popping noise.

"Is that the popcorn?" I asked fearfully.

"Yes."

"Did you decide on a movie?"

The noise stopped and he sat on the couch beside me with a bowl of weird pieces of food. "I have two I'm debating between. Since you haven't seen movies." I watched him eat a piece of the popcorn and then copied him.

It had a weird texture, but was salty and good.

He took a few more bites, walked to a shelf and took something off of it. I guessed it was the movie, but wasn't sure. He sat down and used a different controller to make the movie start on the game console.

"Is it scary?" I asked him.

"No. I think we've had enough scary for today."

At least we agreed on that. I pictured the silver-eyed man again and felt something in me stir. I wondered if I would ever see him again.

We leaned back against the couch and he put the bowl of popcorn between us on the couch. He had chosen one of the drawn cartoon movies and as soon as it started, I couldn't look away. I laughed. I cried. I cheered. And the whole time, Stevens watched me.

When it ended, I sighed. "That was incredible. That poor

lion prince had to endure so much." And parts of it were scary, although not much compared to today's events.

"But it worked out in the end," he reminded me.

"I liked that his girlfriend could pin him," I said with a laugh.

"Most women do."

"I don't think I could pin you," I commented. Stevens looked pretty strong and I didn't.

"I don't think so either," he said with a smirk. "Do you want to watch another?"

I nodded my head enthusiastically. "Yes, please."

"I think you might like this one," he said as he changed the movies.

"I don't know if it will be better than the first one."

"Give it a chance."

I did and I found myself just as mesmerized. "Wow," I said at the end.

"Liked it?"

"I loved it!"

"That's my favorite cartoon."

"What's it called?"

"*Aladdin.*"

"He lucked out with that princess."

"Yes, he did."

"Do you have princesses here?"

He shook his head. "We don't have kings or anything like that here. In other countries they do."

"I don't think you would make a good leader just because you were born from the same family."

"That's very true." I yawned and he asked, "Do you want to go to bed?"

I shook my head. "Can we watch some TV?"

He used the remote to change it and a show about funny

movies came on. We watched short videos of people falling and doing dumb things, which made me laugh. I wasn't sure how it happened, but I ended up falling asleep and Stevens carried me up to my room.

"Stevens," I whispered.

"Troy," he said.

"Huh?"

"My name is Troy."

"I thought it was Stevens."

"Stevens is my last name. My full name is Troy Stevens."

"So I should have a last name?"

"Yes, but it's okay that you don't remember."

"Troy, thank you for helping me."

He pulled a blanket up to cover me and warm me up and said, "You're welcome. I'm glad that I can help you. Sleep well."

CHAPTER SIX

When I woke up the next day the smell of food filled the house. I changed clothes and used the bathroom without screaming when I flushed the weird toilet thing, an accomplishment for me.

"Good morning," I said cheerfully to Troy.

"Good morning, Alys. Did you sleep well?"

I nodded my head. "Did you?"

He smiled and said, "I did."

"What are you making?" I asked him as I watched him mixing a strange liquid like substance.

"Waffles."

I remembered that name from somewhere. "I think I've had those before." My head started to hurt again, so I rubbed at the sides of it.

"Does your head hurt?" he asked me and wiped his hands off on a towel before coming around the stove to put the back of his hand to my forehead.

"Yes."

"No fever. You might just have a headache. I have some medicine for that."

He left the room and I tried to control my heart as it thumped against my chest. I liked him touching me way more than I should have. Even if I didn't have anyone here, I shouldn't be so focused on Troy.

"Swallow these pills with this water," he instructed me, holding out a glass of water and two white ovals.

I did as he asked and nearly gagged as the pills went down my throat. "Thank you." He returned to cooking and a few minutes later someone knocked on his door. "Are you expecting someone?"

He sighed. "No, but that doesn't mean that someone isn't here." He opened the door, but not far enough that I could see the person. "What's up?" he asked whoever was at the door.

"Came to have breakfast," a new man's voice said.

"I'm busy."

"Oh, do you have a girl in there?!" the man asked with excitement.

Troy pushed against the door and then stepped back to reveal a big man with very dark skin. He smiled at me with shockingly white teeth. "Hello."

"Hi."

He walked in past Troy and held out his hand to me. "I'm Drake."

I stared at the hand and looked at Troy. "It's called shaking hands. When you meet someone you do this..." he grabbed Drake's hand and they moved their hands up and down a couple times and then let go of each other. "It's a greeting."

"Dude, she really doesn't know anything."

I held out my hand and Drake shook it. "Nice to meet you, Drake."

"Nice to meet you too, Alys."

"Does everyone know my name?" I asked Troy.

Drake laughed. "Of course! You're the biggest mystery we

have had in a long time. A mysterious, beautiful girl who doesn't remember anything about herself other than her name and age appears in a field."

"Am I supposed to talk to him?" I asked Troy.

He smiled. "Yeah, Drake's my best friend."

"You told her she shouldn't talk to people?"

"No, but he got mad when I was talking to Markston," I explained. "I just didn't want to make him mad again."

Drake's eyes widened and he pushed Troy. "You *dog*."

"He's not a dog," I said in confusion.

"He's just teasing me. You can ignore him," Troy informed me, returning to the kitchen to continue making the waffles.

I sat down at the table and Drake sat in a chair next to me. "So, how are you liking life so far?"

"It's interesting," I whispered. "I did like watching the two cartoons last night. I didn't like the shooting guns or the rude people at the mall."

"Who was rude to you at the mall?" Drake asked. I wasn't really sure that was the part of the story he should be focused on, but I didn't really understand people at all.

"One of those people in the outfits like Troy wears. He said he thinks I'm lying about not knowing who I am."

"It was Barn," Troy informed Drake.

"Oh, well Barn is just jealous."

"Why would he be jealous?" I asked him, seriously confused. "He was mad at me and rude. He didn't seem jealous."

"He only acted like that because he is jealous that Troy is the one who is able to help you."

"So, Barn wanted to help me? He didn't seem like he did."

"He doesn't want to help her. He wants to..." Troy stopped talking and walked to the cold rectangle thing...fridge!

"Troy's the best guy I know. He's the perfect person to help you," Drake said.

"He's been very nice," I agreed.

"Do you want to go to a lake?" Drake asked me.

"That's the big area of water that people swim in, right?" I asked him.

He nodded his head with a big smile. "Yes."

I looked at Troy who was still looking inside the fridge. "Will Troy come?"

"Oh yeah, Troy will come."

"Okay," I said with a smile. "I'll go then."

"You hear that, Troy? She'll go if you go."

Troy nodded his head, but didn't talk. He seemed mad again. Was it me? Was I making him mad about something? I had asked if it was okay to talk to Drake. "Maybe we shouldn't go. Troy doesn't seem like he wants to," I whispered to Drake.

"No, I do. Really," Troy said and smiled at me. The smile seemed forced, but I wasn't going to argue with him. Plus, how had he heard me?

"Perfect!" Drake said loudly. "The lake is my favorite place to go. Sometimes we go fishing, or just sit in inner tubes and float around, or go swimming."

I didn't know how to swim. Hopefully it wasn't mandatory to swim. Drake poured white liquid into three glasses and set them down on the table and then put a plate piled high with waffles on it.

"Do you want some eggs?" Troy asked me.

"Uh, sure," I said without really knowing what he was asking me.

Troy looked at Drake and then said, "I already know you want some."

"Scrambled this time," Drake said, "You broke the yoke the

last three times and that completely ruins it, so you might as well scramble them."

"You could make your own food," Troy told him.

"So, what's your favorite food so far?" Drake asked me, completely ignoring Troy's comment.

"I think burgers, but I haven't had too many types yet."

"We should go to sushi," Drake told Troy.

"I think sushi should be something she experiences a bit later in her dining life," Troy said with a smirk.

"Sushi is the raw fish food, right?" I asked. I wasn't completely sure what it was, but that sounded right.

"Sort of," Drake said, "But it's delicious."

"I like trying new things," I told them. It was fun to learn about all of this stuff.

Troy finished cooking the eggs and set them on the table in a bowl. They were yellow and mushy looking. Troy and Drake each grabbed a waffle, put it on their plates, and put butter and syrup on it. I copied them and ate a bite. It was super sugary and good. I spooned some eggs onto my plate and took a tentative bite. They were okay, but...

"They're better if you put some salt and pepper on them," Troy said and put some on my eggs for me.

"And if you eat them with your bite of waffle," Drake added.

I took a bite of them with just the pepper and salt and was surprised at how much of a difference that made. "That is better." I stabbed some eggs with my fork and stabbed a piece of waffle and tried that. "That's good, too."

"At least she doesn't seem to be a picky eater," Drake commented to Troy.

"You never know, we haven't tried too many things yet," Troy said.

I didn't join in their conversation and instead listened to the friends talk while I ate. They were so comfortable with each other and it seemed like Troy could talk about anything to Drake. Would Troy be able to talk with me like that eventually? Maybe he really didn't trust me. Maybe he never would.

I tried the white liquid and enjoyed it, but didn't ask what it was. Once I was full, I took my plate to the sink and rinsed it off before putting it inside the machine that washed the dishes.

"Thank you for the meal. It was very tasty."

"You're welcome," Troy said with a smile. "I'm glad you liked it."

I went upstairs and could hear Troy and Drake whispering, but didn't stop to try to overhear them. I had learned from a show that that was considered rude. Since we were going to the water I knew I needed to change clothes. Luckily, Gabriella had added a bathing suit to my items purchased at the last second. I wonder if she knew we would be going to the lake. Could she be psychic? The bathing suit was a top and bottom that resembled underwear and a bra, but for some reason the people considered them different. I put that on and stared at my reflection. It was very little clothing covering me. I put on a pair of shorts and a shirt too and tied my hair up so it wouldn't get tangled and look weird after it got wet. When I went back downstairs, Drake was gone and Troy was cleaning the kitchen.

He stopped when he saw me and slowly smiled. "You look ready for the lake."

I nodded my head. "Where'd Drake go?"

"To get his swimming trunks." I had no idea what that meant.

"Troy, I, um..." I stopped talking because I felt silly and nervous. I wasn't sure why I was nervous.

"What's up?" he asked me, dried his hands on a towel and walked out of the kitchen to stand just in front of me.

"I don't know how to swim," I whispered.

"That's okay. We don't have to go swimming."

"I want to!" I blurted out and bit my lip in embarrassment. "Could you, could you teach me?"

"You want me to teach you to swim?"

I nodded my head. "Please."

"Okay, but I'm not really a great teacher."

Happiness surged within me and I threw my arms around him, hugging him tightly. "Thank you!"

His entire body stiffened and I realized I had probably done something wrong. I backed away quickly. "Sorry." I ran up the stairs before he could say anything and shut the door to my room. My heart was racing and I blamed it on the stairs. I couldn't figure out what to blame the sad feeling in my chest on though. I put my sandals on and called myself insulting names the entire time. He hadn't done that when I'd hugged him at the mall. Why now?

I heard his bedroom door close a minute later and then a little bit later someone knocked on the front door and Drake called, "Are you guys ready yet?"

I took a deep breath, tried to forget about the stupid hugging incident, and jogged down the stairs. "I am."

"Here," Troy said to me from the stairs.

I turned and took the towel he held out to me. "Thank you," I whispered and stepped to the side so he could go out the door before me.

Drake looked from me to Troy and then turned and walked towards a large truck. "I'm driving."

Troy stepped outside, but waited to the side of the door. I walked passed him without stopping and climbed into the back seat of the truck clutching the towel that smelled like Troy. He closed his house door and got in the front seat beside Drake.

"We should stop for snacks on the way," Drake suggested.

Troy nodded his head, but didn't say anything. Drake

glanced at me, but I was conveniently looking out the window at everything but the men in the truck with me.

Drake drove faster than Troy usually did and just laughed when Troy chastised him about it. Slowly Troy relaxed and started joking and talking more with Drake. I didn't feel sad about not being included and enjoyed watching Troy talk with his friend. Perhaps we needed Drake over more so Troy wouldn't be so tense with me.

Drake stopped at a place he called a gas station and he went inside the store it had. "Do you want anything?" Troy asked me, turned sideways to get out of the truck but facing me.

I shrugged. "I don't know. Surprise me."

He nodded. "Okay."

He closed the door behind him and I let my head fall back against the window behind me. What was I doing wrong? Why was he acting weird all of a sudden? Clearly, I did not understand men. I didn't think that I had done anything wrong. Why was it okay to hug him before and not now? Troy and Drake came out a bit later with several bags of things. What had they gotten? It looked like a lot. They put them in a blue and white rectangle item in the back of the truck and then got back in the truck and started driving. Was it a secret? Or did they just not think to tell me what they had gotten? I guessed it didn't matter since I would see it at the lake.

We drove for a long time and the scenery changed a lot as we did. When we finally stopped, we were in a forest of trees that smelled a lot better than the place Troy lived. They got out of the truck, so I did too and followed them towards the large, blue lake in front of us. There were several other people there already, but neither guy seemed worried about that. They stopped a short distance from the water and set their stuff down. Then they took off their shirts and I forgot how to breathe. Both were in very good shape, Troy in better shape than Drake except that Drake had bigger arm muscles than Troy.

Drake ran and jumped into the lake and yelled happily when he surfaced. "It's warmer than I thought it would be."

I took off my shirt and shorts and set them on top of my towel, which I set on the sand. When I looked back up Drake and Troy were staring at me. I felt self-conscious and wanted to put my clothes back on, but there were several other girls wearing similar bathing suits to mine and no one seemed to care. I straightened my spine and walked confidently towards the water and tried my hardest to ignore the negative thoughts in my head. I dipped my toes in the water and slowly walked in until the water was up to my knees. Drake wandered a bit away to talk to some women who were swimming near us and soon he had them laughing at something he said. I walked farther into the water and stopped when it reached the middle of my stomach because I was worried about not reaching the bottom and drowning.

"You okay?" Troy asked me softly and swam closer to me.

I nodded my head and then looked around at the lake. It really was beautiful here. Someone was playing odd sounding music and a few women were dancing to it with men drinking and smiling. Out in the water people were riding and driving boats. Some were fishing and others were riding on strange machines that went fast on the water and caused ripples across the lake that reached even to us.

"To keep your head above the water is actually pretty easy," Troy told me, making me look at him. "You just kick your legs back and forth. Watch mine."

The water was clear enough for me to see, so I watched as he slowly moved his feet back and forth under the water. "That's it?" I asked nervously.

He nodded his head. "I'll stay near you, if you want?"

I nodded my head and walked closer to him, the water going up to my chin and then he held out a hand towards me. I set my hand in it and started moving my legs as I pulled my body closer to him by my grip. It seemed to work for a second, but then my head went under the water. Troy wrapped his arm around my waist and lifted me up until my face was out of the water and at the same level as his. I took a deep breath and wiped the water off my face and out of my eyes.

"You okay?" he asked. I nodded my head, but refused to speak. He was holding me right against his body, our chests and stomachs touching. In the water, his skin felt really warm. "Maybe move your legs a little faster this time."

I nodded my head and then he pulled his arm away from my waist. I wanted to throw my arms around his neck, but instead I pushed back from him and moved my legs faster this time and kept my head above the water.

"Good," he said with a smile.

I smiled back, proud of myself.

"To swim, you move your arms like this," he made a weird move where he swung his arm around next to his head and said, "While kicking your feet at the same time. Let's move you back to where you can touch so you can watch me." He pulled me towards the shallower water and once I was on my feet, he started swimming in front of me. "You can try in that water so if you get nervous you can just put your feet down and stand up, okay?"

I felt stupid as I did the arm movements he had shown me and kicked, but he said, "You need to get your feet up towards the top of the water and kick harder." I did, but then I made a lot of noise and splashed water around. "Legs a little lower," he amended.

"Is that guy really teaching her to swim? She's like twenty and she can't swim?" some woman scoffed from nearby.

"What an idiot," another agreed.

"How do you not know how to swim? It's almost natural," a guy agreed.

My face was burning with embarrassment and anger. I probably did know how to swim before. Plus, what was wrong with me learning? If I was supposed to know how, then why was it wrong to learn?

"Just ignore them," he told me.

I continued practicing and managed to swim a bit.

"How's it going?" Drake asked me with a happy smile.

I shrugged and looked down at the water.

"Don't worry about it, we all took lessons as kids," he said. "We took weeks of lessons before we really learned."

I knew he was trying to make me feel better, but it wasn't really working.

"Are you guys hungry? We could start making food," Drake suggested.

"Yeah," Troy told him.

"I'll start the coals," Drake said and walked away.

I was still looking down when a fish swam near me. I stumbled back and Troy laughed softly. "The fish won't hurt you," he said.

"They won't bite?" I asked without looking at him.

"Nope."

I went out into the deeper water and practiced kicking my legs to keep my head above water and watched all of the different people around us. Far off there were some kids playing in the sand and their parents watched them while they sat on towels. As I watched the family I realized two things: one, I wanted a guy who loved me and wanted to do things with me like that; and two, I did not want children.

"You're doing really well," Troy praised me and swam around until he was in front of me.

"I have a good teacher," I said with a smile.

"I think you're just a quick learner."

I shrugged and stopped kicking for a moment which made me drop under the water again. Troy pulled me up quickly and smiled at me as he held me. Everything around us seemed to disappear as I looked into his eyes. He was so nice and sweet and so handsome. I leaned forward to kiss him and he pushed me back until he was holding me by the waist at arm's length.

"Am I ugly?" I asked him as angry tears brimmed in the corners of my eyes.

"What?" he asked with a frown.

"Is that why you won't kiss me?"

"No, it's not that."

"Then what is it? If you're attracted to me then why don't you want to kiss me?" I asked him in confusion. He was single and so was I, so why wouldn't he kiss me? It didn't make sense.

"You're still learning everything and I don't want you to kiss me just because I'm the only man you know right now."

"That's stupid. I've met other men. Is it because you think I'm lying? Is it because you don't trust me still?"

"I don't think you're lying," he said in shock.

I pushed away from him and swam as well as I could until I could touch the bottom. "But you don't trust me," I said angrily and kept walking towards the shore and my towel.

"I didn't say that," he snapped as he followed me.

"Food's almost ready," Drake said with a smile. He was standing next to a round black object that had smoke coming out of it. He saw our faces and his smile wilted. "Everything okay?"

"No," I said angrily.

"Yes," Troy said.

I turned to glare at him and said, "Of course you're fine."

"Alys," he started with a sigh.

"No, I don't want to hear your lies anymore!" I snapped at

him and snatched my towel from the ground. I shook it out, wrapped it around myself and walked towards the building with the symbols that meant there were bathrooms there.

"Alys!" he called after me, but I ignored him and kept walking. I walked past the building and sat at a table around the other side in some grass, which was thankfully deserted.

I put my arms on the table and my head on them and cried. Everything was so confusing and people were mean and rude. Why did people not trust me?

"A man who makes a woman cry isn't worth your time," a man said from in front of me. I lifted my head and gasped at the silver-eyed man sitting across from me. He lifted one of my tears off my face with his finger and examined it. "I don't like seeing you cry, Alys."

"Who are you?" I asked him and sniffled as the tears stopped. For some reason, he made me feel safe.

"I'm a friend," he whispered.

"Do you know me from before?" I asked.

"Before what?" he asked me.

"Before I lost my memory," I whispered to him.

His eyes hardened and the tear disappeared as if evaporated. "That's why you don't recognize me. I thought you were just pretending."

I shook my head. "I don't remember anything, except my name."

He sighed and looked at me sadly. "I wish I could just take you back."

"Back? Back where?"

"I've already said too much," he replied and stood up.

"What's your name?" I asked him, standing up too.

"I can't tell you that," he whispered.

"Why won't you tell me? Why won't you help me with my memories if you know me?" I asked angrily.

"If you saw fit to have your memories removed, then giving them back to you would only cause you to be angry with me. I don't want to make you angry," he explained.

"I had my memories removed? How is that even possible? Why would I do that?" This was so confusing.

"Alys!" Troy called.

"Your *friend* is looking for you," the silver-eyed man growled.

"Wait, please tell me something," I begged him.

"The war is escalating and you might be in danger. As much as I dislike this mortal, he is capable of protecting you for a bit if something happens. Stay with him for now. Stay safe, Alys. Please, stay safe." He rested his fingertips against my cheek and then walked into the forest.

"Who was that? What did he say to you?" Troy asked.

My cheek tingled where he had touched me and I felt sad without him here with me. "A friend," I whispered.

"A friend? He knows you? Wait, isn't that the guy who was bothering you at the mall? How did he find us here? If he's stalking you, I'll..."

"He knows me from before," I told him and looked at him. "Why would someone purposefully forget their memories?" I asked Troy.

"What?" he asked me and was clearly confused by my question.

"He said that I had my memories removed. Why would I do that? What if I'm a bad person? What if I did something terrible?" I asked, my words coming out faster and faster. "Maybe I shouldn't be trusted. Maybe I'm a bad person."

"I don't think you're a bad person," he said.

"You don't know. You don't know me. What if I am a criminal?" I was nearly frantic now.

"If you were a criminal, you would have come up in our database," he said confidently.

"He said there was a war. What war?"

"There are wars all the time," he said, "What else did he say?"

I was near hysterical now and I couldn't make my hands stop shaking. "He said I could be in danger, and that you could protect me and to stay safe. What war? Why would I be in danger? Did I cause the war? Who is it between? Maybe I should leave. I could be putting you in danger and..."

Troy grabbed my arms and squatted down until I could see his face. "You're not going anywhere. If you are in danger, then leaving will only increase the likelihood of you getting hurt. Whatever war this is doesn't matter to me."

"I don't want you to get hurt because of me," I whispered with fresh tears falling down my face for a whole new reason.

It wasn't his fault that he was nice. He shouldn't get hurt just because he was nice.

"It's my job to protect people, remember?"

So now I was just part of his job?

"We're friends, right?" he asked me.

"Are we?" I asked him softly.

He nodded his head and smiled. "Of course we are. And as your friend, I promise to keep you safe, okay?"

"Troy, I don't..."

He stood up and shook his head at me to stop me from continuing what I was going to say. "That's enough. Let's go eat and then we can go back to the house, okay? For all we know, that guy was lying to you and just wanted to make you agitated."

I didn't think the silver-eyed man had lied. He didn't seem like he was lying to me and he seemed like he really knew me. When he realized that I didn't know him, he really seemed sad.

Troy grabbed my wrist and tugged gently. "Come on." I

followed him, but pulled my arm back to cross them over my chest. I was still upset about him not kissing me, but now I wasn't so sure that he was in the wrong.

Drake handed me a plate of food and sat down on his blanket. Troy made a plate and spread his blanket out flat. He patted the open space next to him. "Sit."

I could have sat down in the sand since my towel was still wrapped around me, but I sat next to him and stared at the plate of food. What if there were people following us? Would I be able to tell? Could I lead them away from Troy if I did find them? The man had told me to stay with Troy, but...

"The hot dog is better when it's warm," Drake said around the food in his mouth.

"Dog!" I asked in shock. I didn't know they ate their pets.

"It's not really a dog," Troy explained. "They just call it a hot dog." He pointed to one of the items on my plate. "This."

I picked it up and took a bite. "Juicy," I mumbled as I chewed.

"Thank you," Drake said as though that were a compliment to him.

"What are these?" I asked and held up a weird crisp orange thing.

"It's a chip."

I ate one and on top of the weird crunchiness it was odd tasting.

"Doesn't look like she likes that flavor," Troy said. He handed me a different colored one. "Try this one."

I did. "That one is better."

"Hey, Drake," a woman with huge breasts in a bathing suit that didn't seem big enough said with a smile. "Hi, Troy."

"Hi, Stacy," Drake greeted her with a smile and stood up to hug her.

Troy stood up and hugged her too. "How are you?" he asked her, still standing and facing her.

"I'm good. I was out on the boat and saw you guys so I thought I would come say hi." She was pretty and had a really pretty smile. She looked at me and said, "I haven't seen you before."

"This is Alys," Drake said before Troy could say anything.

I stood up and held out my hand. "Hi."

She shook my hand and said, "It's nice to meet you, Alys. Well, I better get back. If you guys want a ride on the boat, you're more than welcome."

Ride on the boat? That didn't sound fun. "Maybe another time," Troy said and then hugged her again. She hugged Drake again and gave me a weird look before walking towards a rowdy group of people.

"I think her top gets smaller every year," Drake commented and then took a drink of water.

"That's because she keeps getting boob jobs," Troy said and sat down on his towel again. I finished the food that had been on my plate, dropped my towel and went back into the lake.

"She's still mad at me," Troy whispered to Drake.

"Can you blame her? Her first few days of memory haven't been great."

"The guy from the mall who said he would see her again was just here and claims he knows her."

"Does he?"

"I don't know. She seemed to think he might, but she said she doesn't remember. Claims this guy mentioned a war of some kind and that she could be in danger."

"I don't think he's talking about the war overseas."

"Me neither."

"The gangs have been pretty quiet lately. If a war is brewing, it would make sense."

"She doesn't have any tattoos. If she was part of any of the gangs, she would have a mark."

"How do you know she doesn't have any tattoos?"

"The doctor told me. We have to know when we make the found person's report."

"Mmhm."

"Anyways..."

"What if it's the mob? She could be Russian or something."

"That's possible."

"What if she's a mobster's wife?"

"She's a bit young to be anyone's wife."

"You never know."

I walked a bit deeper into the water and moved my arms slowly back and forth through the water.

"She could be a daughter."

"Possible."

"She was really freaked out after that guy left. He told her that she had her memories removed."

"That's not even possible."

"I know, but it really scared her. Now she thinks she could be a criminal."

"Pretty women are usually the best criminals."

"Drake."

"You want me to do some research?"

"Yeah, I'm off for the next week."

"Oh, right. I forgot about that."

"Yeah."

"So, why is she mad at you?"

He sighed loudly. "I don't want to talk about it."

"Don't lose your chance," Drake whispered. "She's pretty and kind and she might never get her memories back. Plus, that guy could be full of crap and just a nutbag."

"I can't."

"Why not?"

"It'd be wrong."

"Wrong? What? You're stupid."

I sat down in the lake, the water coming up to my neck and wiggled my toes around in the sand.

"I need to try to find that guy and question him."

"You need to stop being stupid."

"I'm not being stupid."

"If she's mad at you and you won't tell me the reason, that means you did something stupid."

"Whatever."

"I'll just go ask her myself," Drake said.

"No!" Troy yelled at him. "Drop it, man."

"Hey, Alys!" Drake called.

I turned my head and looked at him. "Yeah?"

Troy tripped Drake who was laughing now. "What's wrong?" he asked me as he stood up and pushed Troy towards the lake and me.

"Huh?" I asked, like I hadn't heard him.

He and Troy were pushing and pulling each other as they walked deeper into the lake. "What's wrong? You seem sad." Drake asked.

Troy shoved Drake, who continued to watch me.

"I don't want to talk about it," I answered him.

"Typical woman response," Drake said. "Really though, what's up? What did Troy do to make you mad?"

"Just drop it," Troy growled and somehow pushed Drake under the water.

He sputtered as he came up and then pushed Troy under the water.

"Are you guys fighting?" I asked him.

"Naw, we're just playing around."

"You're making him mad. His face is scrunched," I whispered to Drake.

He looked at Troy, who was wiping water from his face. "Hey, you're right. Huh? Truce, bro?"

"You done prying?" Troy asked him as he walked towards me and Drake.

"For now."

"You're so damn nosey."

"What does his nose have to do with anything?" I asked.

"It means he asks too many questions," Troy explained.

"So, I'm nosey?" I asked softly.

"No, you're learning about stuff. He's trying to find out information he doesn't need to know."

"So, you don't want him to know why I'm mad, so that makes him nosey?"

"Yeah."

"Why don't you want him to know?" I asked.

"Because he'll make a big deal out of it."

"Why?"

"Because that's what Drake does."

"Why would he care? It doesn't involve him."

"He shouldn't, but he will."

"I am *right* here," Drake said with crossed arms.

"Maybe he could explain your reasoning to me better than you can," I said to Troy defiantly.

He frowned. "No."

I tilted my head back and looked up at the sky to avoid looking at him anymore. He was making me mad all over again. I bet if Stacy had tried to kiss him, he would have let her.

"We should pack up," Troy told Drake.

"Are you ready to go home?" Drake asked.

"Alys, he's asking you," Troy told me.

"Oh, I don't care. I'm just along for the ride," I said as I continued to look at the clouds slowly drifting by overhead.

"Three o'clock," Troy said angrily.

I looked at him with a scowl. "What do you mean?"

"Oh, I see," Drake said, looking off to their right.

"See what?" I asked and turned to look. Jogging down the beach was a woman who had a huge smile on her face and looked like she was headed right for us.

She ran into the water and threw her arms around Troy's neck, making him stumble back a step. "Troy! I haven't seen you in forever."

"Hi, Tara," he replied in a less-than-friendly tone and stepped back from her.

"Alys, you want to help me pack up?" Drake asked me.

I stood up and followed him since it seemed like he wanted to give Troy and Tara some time alone. "Who's she?" I asked him softly.

"That's his ex."

"Ex?"

"The last girl he dated."

"Oh."

I helped put the items in the rectangle thing. "What's this called?" I asked.

"It's an ice chest," he told me.

I glanced back and saw Tara touching Troy's chest as she talked happily to him. He didn't look very happy though.

I dried off with my towel and put my shirt and shorts on again. "Drake, can I ask you a question?"

"Of course," he said with a smile. "You can ask me anything."

"Am I pretty?"

He had picked up a bag of stuff, but set it back down after I asked the question to give me his full attention. "What?"

"Am I pretty or attractive? You know, like Stacy and Tara?"

"No, you're much prettier than them," he said with a smirk.

"Don't lie, Drake. I'm being serious."

"I am too. You're beautiful, Alys. Don't let anyone make you think that you aren't."

Then why wouldn't he kiss me if he had dated Tara and I was prettier?

I turned and saw Tara lean forward, wrap her arms around his neck and kiss Troy on the lips. Anger boiled within me and I turned away just as Troy stepped back from her and met my eyes. "I've got to use the restroom," I mumbled to Drake.

"Alright, we'll wait for you," Drake called from the back of the truck where he was putting the stuff we had brought with us.

I ran to the bathrooms and wished I could scream to release some of my anger. I used the bathroom and then stared at my reflection while gripping the edges of the sink. Even if Drake was right and I was prettier, obviously Troy preferred her to me. Why?

I knew why. It was because of my past. Or lack thereof. Could I blame him for not trusting me when I didn't even know if I was trustworthy?

I washed my hands and headed back to the truck. I didn't want him to come looking for me again. I didn't want to be the girl he had to chase down. Troy and Drake were talking when I came back and Troy looked upset. I didn't even acknowledge either man, climbed into the back seat of the truck, and buckled my seatbelt.

Neither spoke when they got in and I was glad. Their silence didn't last long and soon they were joking with each other. When Drake parked, I got out and went right up to my room. I grabbed some new clothes and took a long hot shower to calm myself down. It didn't work. I got dressed and went out into the backyard and stretched before I began punching and kicking an invisible enemy. It was still hot and without the cool lake water I started sweating immediately. I wasn't sure how I knew the moves or why I was doing them, but I didn't think about it. I punched, kicked, jumped, rolled, and pretended I had a sword. When I was breathing hard and drenched in sweat I sat down in the grass and bent my head forward with my eyes closed. Life was so complicated here. Troy was frustrating and yet I could understand that he couldn't trust me. Yet I still felt angry at him for not wanting me if he did like me.

"Those were some pretty advanced fighting moves," Troy commented from behind me.

"Were they?"

"Yeah."

"Is that a bad thing?"

"Not necessarily. A lot of women learn to fight so that they're not defenseless if a man tries to attack them. Although, I've never heard of one teaching sword fighting before."

"I don't know. It just felt right. The moves just came to me."

"Still no memories?"

I shook my head.

"Would you like to spar with me?" he asked.

"No," I answered immediately.

"Why not?"

I didn't answer him. I didn't want to admit that I didn't want to touch him and I did at the same time.

"I'm sorry that I upset you."

I didn't respond or move.

"Are you going to talk to me?"

"About what?"

"About today."

"Why?

"What do you mean, 'why'?"

"Why would we talk about it? You made it pretty clear that you didn't want to talk about it anymore at the lake. You also made it pretty clear that you preferred Tara to kiss you."

"I didn't want her to kiss me."

"Didn't look that way."

"She's always been pushy. Trust me, I didn't want her to kiss me."

"Why not?"

"Because she and I aren't together anymore and I don't want to get back into a relationship with her."

"So, you don't want a relationship with me," I stated. That made sense. He didn't want to be in a relationship with me so he didn't want to kiss me.

"I didn't say that."

"You, um, interfered, no, inferred it."

"No, I didn't. You're putting words in my mouth."

I turned and stared at him in shock. "I'm nowhere near you or your mouth."

He laughed loud and long. I stood up and brushed myself off before walking around him and into the house. "Wait!" he said and grabbed my arm to turn me around.

"No! You're laughing at me. I'm not going to sit here while you laugh at me." I was crying...again.

He stopped laughing and his face grew serious when he saw the tears and heard my quivering voice. "Alys, I'm sorry. I wasn't laughing at you. I was laughing because of how offended you looked when I said that. It's just a phrase that means you're trying to make it sound like I said something that I didn't."

I pulled my arm out of his hold and stormed up the stairs. "I don't want to talk to you anymore."

"Alys."

"I was wrong about you. I thought you were nice, but you're just like the rest of them. You think I'm stupid and that it's okay to laugh at me. I may not remember much, but I know when someone is being rude," I snapped and then slammed my door closed.

"Alys," he said from outside my door. "Please talk to me. You're just misunderstanding what I'm saying."

"Leave me alone."

He sighed and then I heard him walk down the stairs.

I lay down on my bed and cried into the pillow. I hated this place. Why wouldn't the silver-eyed man just tell me where I was from? Why couldn't I go back? Even without my memories I could go back, right? Or maybe they didn't want me there either.

CHAPTER SEVEN

I couldn't sleep and so I waited until the middle of the night, packed a bag of clothes, took some fruit and water, and as quietly as possible left the house. I wanted to leave a note for Troy, but I didn't know how to write. I walked in the dark night and didn't feel afraid. The cool air brushed against my cheeks like a caress as I started my journey. I had no idea where I was going, but I hoped I could find someplace. I felt sad to leave Troy, but I was convincing myself that it was for the best. If things went sour I had to keep him safe. I wouldn't be able to forgive myself if he or Drake got hurt. Plus, I didn't want to stay with someone who thought it was okay to laugh at me and treat me like that.

Someone was jogging on the opposite side of the street and part of me remembered that people did that to stay in shape. The person came closer and I realized it was Drake. I tried to hide my face, but since I was the only other person outside at this time, he saw me. Before he had time to cross the street I started running at a maintainable pace in hopes that I could out run him and escape.

"Alys!" he yelled after me from nearby.

I increased my speed, running as fast as I could. I turned down random side streets and ran behind buildings, through the alleys.

"Troy, Alys is running. I'm following her right now. We're headed East on Rivers Avenue. Alright."

I wasn't sure how he had gotten a hold of Troy or how he was communicating with him, but I didn't need to know. I just wanted to get away. I turned down another street and saw a dead end ahead. I turned left quickly down the next alley and pushed over a trash can behind me.

"Alys, why are you running? Stop and talk to me," he pleaded.

"Just leave me alone!" I begged him.

"Why are you running?"

"I don't want to get you guys involved in whatever war I'm part of. I'd rather fend for myself." That was only part of the reason I was running. I didn't want to admit the rest to Drake.

"What is the war?"

"I don't know. I don't remember anything."

"Where are you running to?"

"Anywhere but here." I turned down the next street and a car was coming straight at me with bright headlights. I screamed in fear and threw my arms up in front of me. I expected to be hit in the front, but something hit me in the side and I fell to the ground with something on top of me, much less heavy than a vehicle.

"You okay?" Drake asked.

I opened my eyes and realized he had tackled me out of the way of the car. I nodded my head and he stood up off of me with a hand out. I stood up on my own and started walking away again. He grabbed me and held on tight to my arm.

"Let go!" I screamed at him in fear and tried to pull free.

"Alys, let's talk about this," he pleaded.

"No! I don't want to be here anymore. Let me go!"

"We can't just let you leave," Drake told me.

"Why not?"

"If you are in danger, we need to make sure you're safe."

"Who cares! You didn't know me a week ago, so why does it matter now?"

"Because you're our friend," Troy said. I hadn't heard him show up. Had he run here or driven?

I didn't want to see him. "No, I'm not. Friends trust each other and I don't even know if you can trust me."

"That's for us to decide, not you," Troy told me firmly.

"Just let me go. You don't want me here, anyway."

"If I didn't want you here, I wouldn't have taken you from the hospital. Where were you going to go, Alys?"

"I don't know. Far away."

"Were you going to walk the whole way?"

"Yes."

"What were you going to do about food?"

"I wouldn't eat," I said.

"You can't not eat. You'll die."

"Maybe that's better. Maybe I was supposed to die instead of lose my memory. Maybe it's safer that way."

"No one deserves to die," Drake whispered and then dropped my arm.

I rubbed where he had been holding it and sniffed to keep the tears at bay. "What if it all comes back to me and I try to hurt you?"

"You won't do that," Troy said.

"How do you know? If I'm involved in some type of war, I could be crazy."

"If you did have someone take your memories away, then maybe you didn't want to be that person anymore."

"I don't want to be this person, either," I whispered and

wrapped my arms around myself since the night had somehow gotten colder. I was pathetic, mooning over some guy who may or may not like me. It was ridiculous. Troy wasn't the only man in the world.

"Then change. You don't have to stay who you are. People change all the time," Drake told me.

"Come on, let's go back home," Troy suggested.

"I don't want to."

"Why not?"

"Because I don't want to be laughed at anymore!" I yelled.

Troy took a deep breath and said, "I apologized to you for that."

"It doesn't make it hurt less," I whispered without looking at him.

"You laughed at her?" Drake asked him softly.

"No, I laughed at her reaction to something."

"Now I'm cold," Drake complained and rubbed his arms briskly.

"You're the one who chased me," I reminded him.

"If I had let you run off like that, Troy would have killed me."

"Troy wouldn't kill you."

"That just means that he would be really mad at me," Drake explained.

"Why?"

"Because I would be worried about you and spend the next few days searching for you," Troy said.

"You would be worried?" I asked and looked up at him.

He nodded his head. "I would be."

"Why?"

"Because you're my friend. Plus, I'm the one who took you from the hospital so that sort of makes me responsible for you."

"You don't have to be responsible for me."

"I know."

"I'm worried about you," I informed him.

"Because of what that guy said?" he guessed. I nodded my head. "You don't need to be. Drake and I can protect ourselves and each other."

"You're not going to let me leave, are you?"

"Not today," he said with a shake of his head.

I sighed and walked to his car, which I could see parked down the street. Drake got in the car too and we drove back to the house.

"You're pretty fast," Drake commented.

"Maybe you're just slow," I growled with my arms folded across my chest.

"You are pretty out of shape," Troy teased him.

"Speak for yourself. I doubt you would have been able to catch her."

"You only caught me because that car was going to hit me and scared me into stopping," I reminded him.

"A car almost hit her?"

"She ran out into the street from a side alley."

"He tackled me," I whispered.

"Did she hit her head?"

"No, I held it up."

"Maybe my memory would come back if I hit my head," I suggested.

"Or you could give yourself permanent brain damage," Troy said.

"People hit their heads all the time on that funny movie show."

"And most have to go to the hospital," Troy countered.

He stopped in front of his house and I stared at it with tears burning my eyes. I could have made it if only Drake hadn't been out running.

"Thanks for the help," Troy told Drake.

"No problem." He climbed out of the car and when I got out he said, "I live right there." He pointed to a house just across the street. "If you want to get away from Troy, you don't have to run away. You can always just come over to my house."

I nodded my head and walked into Troy's house.

Troy closed the door and I heard him lock it. "Alys," Troy called, making me stop walking up the stairs to my room. "Why did you run away?"

"I told you."

"Are those the only reasons?"

"Why are you so nosey?" I asked.

"Friends are always nosey."

"Or maybe you just think I'm lying and want to find out what I could be hiding."

"Are you lying?"

"No."

"Alys, when Drake called me and told me that you were running do you know what my first thought was?"

I shook my head without looking at him.

"My first thought was that you were in trouble. I thought you were in trouble and running away to try to protect me. I was scared and worried."

Tears brimmed in my eyes, but I refused to let them fall.

"I didn't once think that you were running because you had been lying to us and didn't want me to find out. I didn't once think that I should just let you leave and that I didn't care. I could only think about finding you and making sure that you were safe and bringing you back home."

Why would he think that if he didn't want me?

"Please don't run again, okay?"

"I can't promise that."

"Why not?"

"Because if there is a war and they threaten you, I would rather give myself to them."

"No."

I turned and stared into his hard gaze with my own. "I won't change my mind about that. My life isn't worth as much as yours."

"Of course it is!" he yelled.

"That's how I feel."

"If you did that, it would hurt me. I would feel sad and feel like it was my fault."

"Why?" I asked in shock.

"It's my job to protect you, not the other way around."

"Why? If I can protect you, then why shouldn't I?"

"Because that's not for you to decide."

"That doesn't make sense."

"I know you don't understand, but I don't want you to protect me."

"You never explain anything that I want to know. Why not?"

"I think we're both tired. Why don't we go to bed and we can talk in the morning?" he suggested.

I felt like he was just trying to avoid the conversation, so I went into my room without another word to him. I sat there for a while and then cracked the door open to look out. He was sitting in the hallway in front of his door with his head leaned back against the doorjamb.

"What are you doing?" I asked him.

"Going to sleep."

"Why are you in the hallway?"

"So I will hear you if you try to run away again."

That jerk! How could I leave if he was sitting there? "You're crazy."

"Yup."

"So you're just going to sleep there to make sure I don't run away?"

"Yup."

"What if I never run away again?"

"Then I'll have accomplished my goal."

"Go get in bed."

"Are you going to run away?"

"No."

"How do I know you're telling the truth?"

"I promise I won't run away tonight."

He rolled his eyes at me and didn't move.

"I promise I won't run away during the night."

"Nope."

I sighed and asked, "What do you want me to promise?"

"Promise me that you won't run away ever again."

I could figure out a loophole later. "Fine. I promise I won't run away. Happy?"

"Yes."

He didn't move.

"Aren't you going to go to bed?"

"Nope."

"I promised."

"I know."

"So why are you staying here?"

"To make sure you keep your promise."

I screamed at him and shut my door. "Stupid man."

"I heard that."

"Good!"

THE NEXT MORNING, we didn't talk. I ate the breakfast he had made and sat on the couch to watch TV. Just watching the

TV was helping me learn new words and understand things a little better. None of it helped me understand Troy.

Drake stopped by a little later and Troy went out front to talk to him where I couldn't hear their conversation. I turned the TV up louder and tried to let the funny people ease my foul mood. It wasn't working.

Troy came back in a little while later and sat down on the other end of the couch.

We ate lunch together and then after a few more hours of TV, I fell asleep on the couch. I felt Troy put a blanket on me, but I didn't open my eyes or thank him. I was being rude to him now and I knew that, but I was too mad to care at the moment. I dreamed about wars and being chained against a wall while watching them hurt Troy. I woke up crying, but wiped my face before Troy could see me.

He glanced at me when I woke up and asked, "Do you want something to eat?"

I shook my head and wrapped the blanket around me. What could that dream have meant? Or did it mean nothing and was it just a strange dream?

"Do you want to go watch a movie?"

I shook my head.

"Do you want to play a game?"

I shrugged.

He stood up and went to his room. A minute later, he came down with something in his hands. "I'm going to teach you to play Go Fish."

"I don't want to fish," I told him.

He smiled. "It's not real fishing. It's a card game."

He started to pull out the cards when he remembered something and looked at me. "You can't read the numbers." I shook my head. "Well, I will just have to show you an example when I want something."

"That sounds like a lot of trouble."

"Not really," he said. He began moving the cards between his fingers and making them do weird things. "This is called shuffling," he explained to me. "It's to mix the cards up." He put some cards in front of me and then in front of himself. "Sort them by the symbols at the top," he explained, "So, you see this one?" he held up one to me. "See this symbol? That's a three. Find any more in your stack that have that symbol and hold them together and then do that for the other symbols."

I tried as best as I could and felt flustered at the end of it. "Okay."

"Now, the point of this game is to get all four of one kind. So, if you have four of the same symbols, you put them down like this." He put four cards that had the same symbol down. "I have four fives, so I put them down."

"Okay." I had one set of four too.

"Now we start asking the other person for a card to try to complete our sets. For example, I would say, 'do you have any threes,' which you would then look in your cards to find a three and if you had one you would give it to me and if not, you say, 'go fish'."

"Go fish," I said.

He picked up a card from the stack of cards he had put down earlier. "When you fish you take a card from the deck."

"Do you have any of this?" I turned the card around.

"That's a four. Here." He handed me one.

"Now what?"

"Now I ask again."

I forgot how much time passed or to be mad and as the sun set Troy and I were smiling and happy. I didn't know what my life had been like before, but spending time with Troy made me very happy...most of the time.

"Now I'm hungry," I told him.

"Me too."

He put the cards back in their box and went into the kitchen. I watched him with a smile on my face. "I think I'm going to order pizza," he said after looking in the kitchen a while.

"What does that mean?"

"It means I'm going to call a place that cooks pizza, tell them what I want, and they'll have someone bring it to the house."

"People will bring you food?"

"Yep."

Wow.

"Why don't you do that all the time instead of cooking?"

"It's more expensive than cooking."

"Oh."

"I better order extra because Drake might stop by."

"Is he mad at me?" I asked.

"I don't think so."

"Good."

"Do you want to talk about yesterday?" he asked me. "Before Drake gets here?"

I did, but I didn't. "No." I really didn't want to ruin the night.

"You sure?"

I nodded my head.

"Okay, I'm going to order the food."

"Can we get cheesesticks?" I asked.

"How'd you know about those?"

"There was a guy talking about them on the TV."

"Oh, a commercial. That's when they advertise items so people will want to buy them."

"It works."

"Yes, it does. Sure, I haven't had cheesesticks in a long time."

I relaxed on the couch and watched more TV. Troy talked

to someone on the phone about pizza and then as soon as he said bye his phone rang. He walked outside as he answered, "Stevens."

Was it his work? It seemed like only people at his work called him by his last name.

The door opened and instead of Troy, Drake walked in. "Hey."

"Hi, Drake."

"How are you?"

"Fine. I learned Go Fish today."

"Oh, and did you like it?"

"It was fun. We're getting pizza."

"Really? Well I came at the perfect time then."

"Drake, what's alcohol?" People talked about it and drank it a lot on the TV shows.

"It's a drink that can mess with your head."

"Then why do people drink it?"

"Some people like the taste. Some people like the way they feel after drinking it."

"Do you drink it?"

"Sometimes."

"Can I try some?"

"You're not old enough to drink it."

"What?"

"You have to be twenty-one."

"Oh."

Troy came back inside and Drake said, "You know, even when she turns twenty-one, she won't be able to drink anywhere."

"What?" Troy asked, clearly caught off guard by the topic of our conversation.

"Since she can't get an ID, she won't be able to drink anywhere."

"Or drive," Troy added.

"That's not fair," I complained.

"Well, it's the law unfortunately."

"I don't like that law."

Troy smiled and said, "A lot of people don't like the laws."

"Why can you guys drink and I can't?"

"Even if you had ID, you can't drink because you're too young."

"That's dumb."

Troy shrugged. "Sorry, I didn't make the laws, I just enforce them."

"What was the call about?" Drake asked him.

"They cleared me for work. Turns out there were cameras and they had enough witnesses to clear me without even needing a trial."

"That's crazy. I've never heard of that happening before," Drake said.

"Does that mean you get to get your gun back?" I asked him.

He nodded his head. "And I'll be going back to work."

"So I'll be here alone?" I asked nervously.

"We'll think of something," Troy promised me.

"What kind of pizza did you order?" Drake asked to change the subject.

"Don't worry, I got your favorite for you."

"Have I ever told you that you're my best friend and awesome?"

"Not enough," Troy teased him.

"You want a hug?" Drake asked and opened his arms.

"No."

"Troy doesn't like being touched," I said without meaning to. I pressed my lips together and stared at the TV.

"Oh, the mystery starts to unfold," Drake said.

"Shut up, Drake. And that's not true," Troy said.

Right, you just don't like me touching you. Thankfully, I didn't say it out loud this time. "I beat Troy at Go Fish," I told Drake instead and hoped they would let the topic change.

"He loses every game he plays," Drake told me.

"I beat you at horseshoes last picnic," he said.

"I was drunk."

"I still won."

"What's drunk?" I asked them.

"That's when you've had too much alcohol," Troy told me. "It makes you stupid."

"Hey we should go see that new movie," Drake said with excitement. He must really want to see it.

"I don't know. It's a lot of action."

"That's fighting, right? I like those movies," I told Troy. "Unless you don't."

"What action movies have you seen so far?"

"There was a movie called *Rocky* and *Kickboxer*."

"See, she's fine."

"Alright," Troy relinquished.

"Awesome!" Drake said happily.

The doorbell rang and Troy went to answer it. "What's this movie about?" I asked.

"It's about people with super powers."

"What's that?"

"Like extra abilities. One guy can fly and another can change shape."

"Wow."

"Just wait until you see it. It looks real."

"Movies aren't real though, right?"

"Right," he agreed with a nod, "but the advancement of technology has made it so as you're watching it, you really believe that it's happening."

"I wish I could fly," I whispered.

"Most humans wish to fly," Troy said as he took boxes from a young guy who was staring at me. Troy noticed and said, "Have a good day," and then shut the door in his face.

I didn't comment on his behavior and was saved by the pizza being there. We put slices of pizza and cheesesticks on plates and sat at the table to eat before we went to the movie. Drake and Troy talked about work and I couldn't follow along with their conversation so I became lost in my own thoughts.

What if the silver-eyed man was a liar? What if he *was* just some crazy guy who saw my picture and heard my story and wanted to mess with me? Part of me wanted to believe that, but another part of me felt some weird connection to him. It was so strange and so difficult to explain. I had drawn a few pictures of him, but I hid them from Troy because I was certain that he would get upset if he saw them.

"Alys. Alys!" Troy yelled.

I jerked back in surprise and Drake chuckled. "Sorry, what did you say?"

"Are you ready to go to the movie?" Troy asked with a scowl.

I pushed my empty plate towards the center of the table and nodded my head. "Sure."

"Let me go grab my wallet real quick," Drake said and quickly left the house.

"Are you okay?" Troy asked me with pinched eyebrows.

I nodded my head and went to the couch to put on my shoes.

"You want to talk about whatever it is you were thinking about?"

"I was just thinking about the silver-eyed man," I admitted to him.

"Oh?"

"I want to believe he was just crazy, but I don't think he is. I think he was being honest."

"We have some guys looking into it for us. Hopefully, we will have some answers tomorrow."

"If I am some mobster's daughter, will that make you hate me? Since you're a cop?" I asked him softly while staring at my hands.

He sat down next to me and whispered, "I won't ever hate you, Alys."

"If I'm a bad guy, you're supposed to hate me. Cops aren't supposed to like bad guys."

"Cops don't have to hate bad guys. Plus, even if you're the daughter of some mobster or gangster, it doesn't mean you're a bad person."

"Part of me hopes we never find out who I was before."

"I think the most important thing is that you figure out who you are now."

"I'm not a very good person right now. I need to change," I whispered more to myself than to him.

"You're a great person. You just got scared and that's normal. Everyone gets scared occasionally."

I snapped my head up to look at him. "Even you?"

He smiled and nodded his head. "Even me."

"What scares you?"

"There are a few things, but I was scared when you were running. I was scared that you might get hurt. If that truck had hit you, I would have been very scared about your life."

"I was scared when I saw it," I whispered. "I'm sorry that I scared you."

"That pizza guy was pretty interested in you," Troy whispered.

"I saw."

"It was rude of me to slam the door in his face."

"Why did you?" Not that I wanted him to stare at me like he was.

"I didn't like the way he was staring at you."

"You told me that men were going to stare at me, remember?"

"It doesn't mean that I will be okay with it."

"Why not?" He wasn't making sense.

He sighed and then met my gaze. "Because I've grown to like you much more than I should in these few days."

"What does that mean?" I asked nervously.

"It means that I think you're beautiful, smart, kind, and that I've been doing everything in my power not to do this..." He leaned towards me and every cell in my body began tingling nervously. I had seen this in movies and I wanted him to do it to me. Our lips were about to touch when feet stomped up the front porch. Troy leaned back, stood up, and faced the kitchen. Why had he stopped?

"Troy," I whispered in confusion.

Drake threw open the door and asked, "Are you guys ready?"

"Yeah," Troy said sadly. "Let's go."

What? He was just going to leave like that? He wasn't going to finish what he had started?

"Who's driving?" Drake asked.

I wrapped my arms around myself and walked out of the house without looking at either of them. I would not cry. I would not cry. I was not sad. Chin up.

"What's up with her? Something happen?" Drake asked Troy.

Troy didn't answer his question, "You should drive."

I walked to Drake's truck and leaned my forehead against the passenger-side door. I felt sad even though Troy had admitted that he liked me. If he couldn't kiss me then maybe he didn't really mean it. Maybe he didn't want Drake to see us kiss because he would be embarrassed. Drake pressed a button to unlock the truck's doors and I opened mine as fast as possible so I could get in before Troy caught up to me.

We drove listening to their music and I finally calmed down enough to ask, "Is there anything I should know before going to this movie?"

"Do you know what Norse Gods are?" Drake asked me.

"No." It was tingling some memory in my head, but it wouldn't come out.

"There are lots of religions from all over the world," Drake informed me, "and the Norse were one of them. Their main gods were Odin, Thor, Loki..."

I couldn't hear him anymore. My head was pounding so hard and so loudly that it was the only noise I could hear. I clutched at my skull and tried to rub the pain away, but it wasn't working. Drake was still talking, but instead of hearing him, I could hear words of other men. They didn't make sense or form complete sentences, but I could hear their voices. They seemed familiar and friendly. Faces including the silver eyed man flashed across my closed eyelids. Who were they? What did this mean?

"Alys?" Troy asked me, his voice finally breaking through. "What's wrong?"

"My head hurts," I whispered.

"Drake, stop at the gas station over there," Troy ordered him. Drake obeyed and Troy hopped out of the truck as soon as we stopped.

"I wonder if we should take you to the hospital? This is the second time you've gotten a bad headache like this."

"I don't want to go to the hospital."

Troy got back in the truck and handed me a cold bottle of water. "Drink that while I open the pills." I drank while he worked on getting me two white pills and then I swallowed those down.

"Thank you," I whispered.

"Maybe we shouldn't go."

"No!" I yelled. "I want to go watch the movie. These pills usually help."

"Alright."

We drove again and I drank the rest of the water before we got to the theater. There were quite a few people around so I stayed close to Troy's side. Why were there so many people here? Did everyone really like watching movies that much? We had to maneuver around people and for a second, I lost sight of Troy. Panic began to set in and I was about to yell his name when he squeezed between two people in front of me. "Hey, come on."

"I lost you," I whispered.

He linked our fingers together and tugged gently. "Stay close to me, okay?"

I nodded my head and tried to stay right next to him as we walked. Drake was waiting for us at a doorway and handed me a ticket. "Hand this to the guy up there."

I walked in and handed the guy, who looked super bored, my ticket. He tore it in half and said in a monotone voice, "Theater seven on the left." Troy and Drake were told the same thing and then we started walking towards the left side.

"There are so many people here," I whispered. Someone tried to cut between Troy and me, but I pressed myself to his side and the person swerved around us. Troy put an arm around my shoulders and held me closer to him as we walked. It felt like it was intimate, but I knew it was just to keep me from getting lost.

We entered through a door, walked down a dark hallway

and then there was a huge TV screen on the wall in front of us. "That's a huge TV," I whispered.

"That's why we come here to watch movies. The screen is huge and the sound is better," Drake said. They led me up through a bunch of seats until they found the ones they wanted and sat down.

People began filing in and filling up the seats and before they turned on the show the entire theater was filled. I felt nervous with so many people around that I didn't know, but thankfully I was sitting between Drake and Troy. I wished we were still holding hands, but he had let go as soon as we found the seats. The lights turned off and it began. First there were commercials and then I felt like I was dreaming. The images felt so real and it really did seem like the guys had the unusual powers. How did they make movies like this?

Halfway through the movie I felt irritated. "Loki isn't like that," I hissed. "And neither is Thor." They didn't look like thirty-year-olds. They both looked like they were my age. I knew they were really older than that, but they aged very slowly so at their current states they looked to be my age. And Thor didn't love Loki and Loki wasn't Odin's son and didn't have the possibility to run Asgard.

Oh, Asgard! How beautiful it looked in real life. They almost captured it in the movie, almost. My head hurt once more when I realized that I shouldn't know any of this and then the pain released and all of my memories came flooding back to me.

Tears streamed down my face and I felt the two halves of me merged into one. I knew that there was no way I could tell Troy where I was really from or anything about my past. They wouldn't believe it. No one would believe me. They would think I was crazy.

"Are you okay?" Troy whispered to me.

I nodded my head and stared at this kind mortal beside me. It was because of him that life on Midgard hadn't been horrible. I owed him a great debt. How could I repay him?

Something exploded above our heads and Troy and Drake pushed me down and covered me with their bodies. People screamed in shock and then everyone became silent. We sat back up and I stared in shock at a group of Dark Elves on the floor in front of the screen. They were scanning the audience and I recognized the one in the center. He was the one who had come to Asgard and talked to me. He met my gaze and smiled. "Alys of Asgard, we have come for you."

"Did he just say her name?" Troy asked Drake.

I swallowed the lump in my throat as I stood up. I couldn't let them hurt the humans. "What do you want with me?" I asked them. How had they found me?

"Is this part of the movie? Is this like an extra from the theater?" someone in the audience asked.

"You idiot, they wouldn't destroy their ceiling," someone snapped.

"We are in need of a negotiating chip and you will help us win the war," the Dark Elf said with a sneer.

"I won't help you defeat the Aesir," I told him defiantly.

Fire crackled around him and he asked, "Maybe if I kill a few mortals, your mind will change?"

"Alys, what's going on? Do you know these guys?" Troy asked.

"They're Dark Elves," I whispered. "Evil beings who only like to hurt and kill."

"We need to get these people out of here," Drake said.

"Just stay put," I ordered them. "They want me."

Troy grabbed my arm. "You promised you wouldn't run away again."

I turned to face him and smiled. "I'm not running away,

Troy. I'm leaving willingly with them." I kissed him on the lips and while he was standing there dumbfounded, I leapt over the seats and ran out the emergency exit.

"After her!" the Dark Elf leader bellowed.

I dodged and weaved through the crowds and made it to the back where the parking lot was empty. The Dark Elves surrounded me and I felt their evil like a chill up my spine.

"Alys!" Troy yelled from the theater.

"What are you going to do to me?" I asked the leader.

"Oh, don't you worry about that. You will find out soon enough."

The elves ran at me and I tried my best to fight them back, managing to hold my own against a few of them, but then one hit me in the jaw and I stumbled to one knee. Another kicked me in the side and I screamed in pain.

"ENOUGH!" a deep voice bellowed and suddenly the air was electrified. The elves went flying in all directions and there, in the center of them, stood Thor with Mjölnir in his hand.

"Thor," I whispered in shock. "What are you doing here?"

He looked at me and said, "I told you that I would protect you."

The Dark Elf leader charged Thor and he narrowly avoided the wicked-looking sword the elf tried to cut him with.

Warm arms picked me up and I smiled at Loki and his silver eyes. "It was you," I whispered.

"I promised you that I would follow you across the nine worlds," he reminded me.

I set my hand on his cheek and jerked it back as pain bit into me. "Loki, what's happened?" I stared into his eyes and saw the well of darkness with no light anywhere. "No. Loki. No."

He refused to look at me anymore and said, "I'm taking you back to Asgard."

"No!" I leapt out of his arms. "I can't go back."

"It's your home!" Loki yelled at me. "Why can't you go back?"

"My home is Midgard. I am upsetting the balance of the Aesir by being there. I'm a mortal, Loki, I'm not meant to be with a God."

He slipped his hand around the base of my neck and stared into my eyes. "I don't give a damn about the balance." He kissed me and pain pricked me all over from the darkness he carried, but I didn't try to stop him.

Loki pulled back and instantly pushed me down. I thought he was being cruel until I saw the sword fly over our heads. He pulled his sword and began fighting with the other elves who had returned from being sent flying by Thor's attack. Thor was still fighting the leader and I was helpless to do anything, but watch.

"Alys!" Troy yelled from nearby.

"Mortal, take her to safety," Loki ordered him.

I stood up and looked at the two gods battling the Dark Elves. What if they didn't win? What if...

"Alys," Thor whispered from nearby as he fought the leader. "Go with them. We will find you soon."

"Thor, I'm sorry."

He smiled and said, "You did what you thought was right. You did what you thought was best for us. It has only made you shine brighter in my heart. Go."

I stood up and ran towards Troy and Drake who were staring at the scene in shock. "We need to get away from here," I told them. "I know you're supposed to keep the peace here, but you can't help them. Thor and Loki will send them away from Midgard, Earth, but we have to get out of here while we can."

"We're hallucinating, aren't we?" Drake asked Troy.

Troy shook his head and looked at me in shock. "You know them?"

I nodded my head. "My memories came back during the movie. I can explain everything at the house."

One of the Dark Elves started to run towards us and Thor threw Mjölnir into the elf's head, knocking him out. "Go!" he shouted at us.

"No, Alys, come to me," the leader of the Dark Elves commanded.

My body twitched and then I was walking towards him. I couldn't stop. I couldn't control myself.

"Alys!" Loki yelled as he fought with one of the Elves. "Fight it! Fight his command!"

Troy grabbed my hand and tried to hold me back. "Alys, what are you doing?"

"Kill him," the Dark Elf ordered me.

No! My free arm lifted and then punched Troy in the face. He stared at me in disbelief.

Thor started attacking the leader to break the spell, but it was no use. I kneed Troy in his stomach and punched him in the jaw again. Drake grabbed my other arm and held me.

"She's being controlled," Drake growled.

"Obviously," Troy said as he held me. "Alys, you can fight this. He can't control you completely."

How? How did I fight it?

"Kill them!" the Dark Elf bellowed at me.

Somehow, I pushed both Drake and Troy away and grabbed a sword from one of the fallen Elves. Loki stepped into my path and the sword lowered towards his chest. No! No, not Loki!

"Alys," he whispered.

The sword's tip stopped, barely a breath away from his chest.

He smiled and twisted my wrist to make me drop the sword. I pushed against the wall of power in my mind that was no doubt the Elf and fell to my knees.

Loki hugged me tightly. "I told you that you wouldn't hurt me."

"Loki," I cried.

He kissed my cheek and set me on my feet next to Troy. "Go, go to safety and we will find you once we send them away from Midgard."

I grabbed Troy's hand and pulled. "Come on!" I didn't want him to take control of me again.

He finally started walking, and before long we were in Drake's truck and then home. We sat at the dining table and I took a deep breath. "Most of this you won't believe," I told them, "but it's the truth. I was born here, but there is no record of my birth because Odin took me to Asgard shortly after I was born. I'm not sure the whole story, but I know my parents died and Odin didn't want me to die as well, so he took me to his home. I lived on Asgard and was raised with Thor and Loki and the other gods up there. I realized that I was causing them to be unbalanced because instead of Thor and Loki trying to convince one of the goddesses to be their wives, they were trying to court me. I had Sif erase my memories and Heimdall sent me to Midgard."

"You were raised with gods and goddesses?" Drake asked.

"Yes."

"And Thor and Loki were trying to date you?" Troy asked.

"Yes." I felt uncomfortable talking about them with Troy, but I had to be honest with him.

"So you ran away from them because the gods were trying to date you?"

"In a sense, yes."

"You realize that is every girl's wish here? They all would kill for a chance to date one of them?" Drake asked.

"Yes, but they don't really know them. They don't know what it's like."

"Are they bad? Is Loki a bad person?"

He was turning dark. I could feel it in him. "No, they are good."

"So why wouldn't you want to date them?"

"I told you! I was ruining the balance. I should never have been brought there."

"So you came here to start a new life," Troy said. "But now those things want to kidnap you."

"There's a war starting between the worlds and they wanted to use me as a bargaining chip. They know that the Aesir are fond of me."

"We are not *fond* of you," Thor snapped. "We love you. You are a Daughter of Asgard and our friend."

He had just appeared out of thin air in the living room which spooked Drake and Troy into standing up and preparing to fight. I stayed in my chair and sighed. "Thor, how many times do I need to go over this?"

He squatted down next to my chair and brushed my cheek with his knuckle. "I don't care about the balance, Alys. I want you to come home. We miss you. Odin misses you."

"Odin knows it's for the best."

Thunder rumbled and lightning sizzled around Thor. "This isn't the best for me."

I ran my fingers through his golden hair, which was longer than usual. "You are meant to be with Sif," I told him softly as tears slid down my cheeks. "And I am meant to live here on Midgard."

"Is it this mortal?" he asked and looked at Troy. "You think this mortal will make you happy?"

"Whether it's Troy or another, I don't know, but I do know that I do not belong on your world."

"Repeating it over and over again won't make it true," Loki

said as he appeared behind Thor with a scowl and stood with his arms folded across his chest.

I walked to him and stared into his angry eyes. "I know you're mad at me. You have every right to be mad at me. I lied and ran away without saying goodbye. In my defense, you never would have let me go otherwise."

"I'm taking you back," he told me and grabbed my arm, "You're going home with me."

I reached up slowly with my free hand and placed my fingers against his temple and cheek. "Odin gave me a bit of power when I was younger to try to help me survive you all. I'm going to use it now."

"Alys, no!" Thor yelled.

"What are you doing?" Loki asked as I froze him in place. It wouldn't last long, but then again this wouldn't take long to do.

"Taking some of your darkness back and giving you some of my light. You mustn't let the light within you fade. You must never let your light fade."

"No," he said in shock and struggled against the spell I had used to freeze him.

"You must live your life on Asgard and find a wife," I told him, "but I will live on Midgard and I will be your light no matter who you take as a wife." I opened the well within him and then opened myself up. The darkness recoiled from my light at first, but after a gentle coaxing it began to flow between us and soon Loki and I were half light and half dark. My body hurt and I felt the darkness trying to take over and consume me, but my light was too great for it to conquer.

Loki caught me as I fell and cradled me against his chest. "You foolish woman."

"It's the least I could do after all of the times that you've saved me," I whispered.

"The Dark Elves could come back," Thor warned Troy and Drake. "They're susceptible to iron."

"How do we kill them?" Troy asked Thor.

"You can't."

"What?"

"They're immortal like us so only we are able to kill them. The only thing you can do is hurt them enough to make them leave. We will be hunting them tomorrow after we speak with Odin."

The pain subsided and I was able to stand on my own again. "Loki, can I have a weapon please?"

"You shouldn't fight," Thor argued.

"You could be far away in a battle and unable to reach me in time," I told him.

Loki opened his palm and a sword appeared in it. "This is my blade of darkness. It should cut through them."

"You can't walk around carrying a sword," Troy told me, "It's against the law."

"I won't be going anywhere, so I will only have it by my side here and that isn't against the law."

Loki tilted my chin up to look at him. "If you're in trouble, you call for me, do you understand?" I nodded my head and then he kissed me lightly on the lips. I should have felt bad for Troy seeing me kiss him, but I shoved that thought aside and allowed myself this moment with Loki since there would not be more. "No matter what happens in the future, I will always love you, Alys."

"I will always be your light, Loki, no matter what I do here."

Loki looked at Troy and said, "You treat her like a Princess, because that is exactly what she is." He disappeared and Thor walked over to me with a scowl.

"I'll be alright," I told him softly. "This is for the best for everyone."

"I will listen for your call. Anytime that you need me, I will be here."

"You give me too much," I whispered to him.

He kissed me deeply and said, "I would give you the nine worlds if I could."

"I will cherish your friendship for the rest of my life."

"This isn't goodbye," he told me. "I will visit you again."

"Thor," I whispered.

He put his finger on my lips and said, "I will abide by your decision, but only if I may visit you once a month."

I would have to try to make him shorten his time, but for now I nodded my head. "Okay."

He kissed my forehead and turned to Troy. "Keep her safe. She's Asgard's most beloved treasure."

He disappeared and I shook off the lightning sizzling along my body and tried to slow my heart, which was beating abnormally fast.

"Well, that was interesting," Drake whispered.

Troy looked mad and I couldn't blame him. "If you want me to leave, I understand," I told Troy softly.

He stormed up to his room and slammed the door closed. I flinched and felt sad and angry at the same time. The darkness was going to take some getting used to as it tried to take over my feelings and actions.

"Just give him some time," Drake told me. "This is a lot to take in."

"Thanks, Drake."

He left and I went to my room to rest. I had a feeling that the Dark Elves would be back sooner than we wanted them to and I needed to do be ready for them when they came.

CHAPTER EIGHT

The next day, Troy was gone and when I woke, found Drake watching TV in Troy's living room.

"He's avoiding me, isn't he?" I asked, my shoulders slumped in defeat. I found a nice guy and now he wasn't even talking to me.

"Yeah, but he'll get over it soon," Drake said with a smile.

"Why is he so mad at me? I didn't lie. I didn't remember any of that until we were in the movie."

"How would you feel if you were in his shoes?" Drake asked me.

"I wouldn't be mad at him."

"You wouldn't be upset that two goddesses were vying for the guy you liked? You wouldn't feel like you had no shot?"

"I turned them both down and told them I wasn't going to Asgard," I reminded him.

"Yes, but Troy is not a god and feels that he is nothing when compared to beings like Loki and Thor."

"I'm not a goddess, either." He wasn't making any sense. Why would Troy be upset? I had turned Thor and Loki down. I had told them to go find wives.

"He doesn't think he can compete with them. He doesn't think he will be good enough for you. In his mind, there is a possibility that you will go back with them if they can manage to convince you."

"That's absurd!" I yelled and threw my hands up in the air. "Why are men so ridiculous?"

Drake laughed and said, "Women aren't exactly normal or levelheaded, either."

I put my head on the table and said, "Maybe I should just leave."

"He doesn't want you to leave, trust me. I've been his best friend most of our lives. He's just trying to deal with all of this right now. Give him some time to work himself out and he'll be fine."

"I need to find a job."

"I think I might be able to work on that for you, but I need to talk to Troy and some people at work first."

"Really?" I asked excitedly.

"Don't get your hopes up; it's just an idea right now."

"I need to figure out some way to repay Troy," I told him.

"He wouldn't want you to repay him."

"I have to."

"Well, I'm sure you'll think of something," Drake said.

I stopped talking about Troy and we lapsed into silence as we watched TV. Drake fell asleep so I turned the TV to a cooking channel. Maybe I could learn to cook and that would make Troy happy. If only I could understand their symbols. "Sif, why couldn't you have given me the ability to read and write their symbols too?"

"You didn't ask me for that," Sif said from across the room.

"Sif!"

Drake stirred but didn't wake up.

"Thor and Loki told Odin what happened here," she

informed me. "I'm surprised your memories came back without the phrase I set it for."

"So, can you teach me to read and write their symbols?" I asked hopefully.

"You're certain that you're staying here?" she asked me softly.

"Of course I am. You're the one who has been trying to get me to leave my entire life. Why are you asking me this now?"

She frowned and said, "Asgard isn't the same without you there. Thor and Loki are depressed and Odin hardly talks to anyone. Even I miss you. It's too quiet."

I smiled and said, "In time, things will return to normal. You and I both know that this is the proper course."

"Alright," she said with a sigh. She put her hands on my head and after a brief stab of pain, I felt nothing different.

"Are you sure you did it right?" I asked her.

She glared at me and put her hands on her hips. "Are you questioning my abilities?"

I picked up a magazine that I had been looking at the pictures of mainly and gasped when I realized that I could read the articles. "You're amazing, Sif."

"I know. It's about time you figured it out."

I hugged her and whispered, "Watch their backs for me, please."

She nodded her head and then hugged me back. "You'll always be a Daughter of Asgard, Alys. And perhaps, in time, you could come visit there."

"I would like that."

She disappeared and Drake asked, "Who was that? She was beautiful."

"That was the Goddess Sif."

"Did she hurt you?"

"No, she came to grant me an extra ability," I told him with a smile.

"What was that?"

"It's a surprise."

I watched the cooking show a bit longer and then went to the kitchen to attempt to make dinner. Drake watched me in silence and only left when Troy came home.

"Welcome home," I called as I took down plates and set the table.

Troy didn't answer me and walked up the stairs to his room. A little bit later I heard the shower turn on. I put the food I had made in bowls and set them on the dining table and then poured us each a glass of water and set that on the table too. I ran upstairs and changed into the dress Troy had purchased for me and braided my hair as neatly as I could and then ran back downstairs.

I was just pulling the cake out of the oven when Troy came downstairs. "Dinner is ready," I informed him. He walked into the kitchen and stared in shock at the dining table. "I hope it tastes good," I told him. "I followed the directions, but it was my first time making it."

"You made this?" he asked with shock as he looked at the food.

I nodded my head.

He looked over at me and his eyes widened, but he didn't comment on my appearance. I tried to hide my hurt feelings and sat down at the table. Troy sat down and took a deep breath. "It smells really good." I smiled proudly and watched as he made his plate and took a bite. "This is really good."

"Thank you," I said with a smile. "I worked really hard on it." I made my own plate and we ate in silence for a bit. "How was your day?" I asked him softly.

"Fine."

"That's good."

"Where's Drake?"

"At home. I asked him to give us some space tonight so that we could talk."

Troy set his fork down and scooted his chair back a little bit to cross his arms over his chest. "Talk about what?"

"Everything," I whispered.

"I don't really know what to talk about or where to start," he said and looked at his plate of food.

I had to talk to him now or I would lose my nerve. As much as I was terrified of his response, I had to find out what he was thinking. "I lived on Asgard my entire life. I came here because a mortal shouldn't live there. A mortal should live here. I made my choice to leave Thor and Loki and my father, Odin, behind. I came here to make a fresh start for myself. I'm sure everything came as a big surprise to you, especially since most people here don't believe in the Gods anymore. I'm sure seeing Thor and Loki kiss me and say those things was upsetting to you, just like it was upsetting for me to see you and Tara kiss. However, I'm not dating them and never was, just like you heard me tell them. I am going to live here on Midgard and make my own life. If you don't want me to live here, that's fine. I will find somewhere else to live. If you don't want to be friends anymore..." I took a deep breath to calm the emotions just saying these things caused, "... then I understand. I hope that isn't the case, but I will not force you to do anything or force you to let me stay here. I may not have been raised here, but this is my rightful home and I will find a place whether it's with you or not."

"Where would you go?" he asked me.

I shrugged. "There are homeless shelters for women that I could go to. I'm sure that I could find something out there. Or I could live in the wilderness for a while. I've been trained to survive in the mountains."

"You're going to live in the mountains?" he asked me doubtfully.

"If I have to."

"And if I told you that I wanted you to stay here?" he asked.

I smiled. "Then I would stay here and try to find a way to repay you."

"You don't have to..."

"I know I don't, but I owe you and that's that. So before you decide, let's eat dessert and have one last happy night together, okay?"

He nodded his head, but now he was scowling. I put the frosting on the cake while he finished eating and then set the cake on the table. "You made this?" I nodded my head. "Where'd you learn how to do this?"

"I was granted the ability to read and write as a final boon for moving back here. So, I followed the directions in the cookbook you have. I wanted to make what could be our final night together a memorable one."

I cut the cake and handed him a slice of it. He ate it and I tried to eat mine, but only managed to eat half because it was very sugary. I started cleaning the table, but when I reached for his plate, he grabbed my hand and stood up. "Are you sure that you want to live with me?" he asked. "I'm going to go back to work and I'll be away a lot. We might not see each other that often."

"This is your choice. I've already made mine," I told him in as steady of a voice as I could manage.

He slid his arm around my side and pulled our bodies together. "I couldn't bear to see you leave. I would chase after you just like I did that night. I meant it when I told you that your past didn't matter to me. I just needed a day to clear my head and wrap it around everything that had happened."

"So, I can stay?" I asked hopefully.

He kissed me deeply and said, "You can stay with me as long as you like."

"That's a bold offer. What if you end up disliking the new me?"

"Will you go out to dinner with me tomorrow?" he asked me.

"Sure, where are we going?" I asked happily.

"No, I mean will you go on a date with me?"

"A date? Like boys and girls do?" I felt shaky all over. Living together and kissing occasionally was one thing, but to be an official couple...

"Yes, a date as a couple."

"You want us to be a couple?" I asked breathlessly.

He smiled and said, "I do."

I wasn't sure what to say at first. This was shocking and exciting and amazing. "Yes, I'll go on a date with you." He kissed me again and I felt tingly all the way to my toes. I wrapped my arms around his neck and kissed him back. "Does this mean you like me better than Tara and Stacy?" I asked him.

"It means that I like you better than every woman on Earth." He told me and kissed me again.

We walked to the living room and sat on the couch kissing until I fell asleep with him holding me. Everything felt like it was falling into place and I felt happy. Part of me mourned Asgard and my friends, but I had hope that I could visit again once the balance was returned.

Something exploded nearby and Troy was instantly alert and covering my body with his. I lifted my head and fear constricted my heart at the sight of the Dark Elves in the doorway. Troy stood up and aimed a gun at them. I had no idea where he had pulled it from, but it gave me a moment to reach under the couch and grab my sword.

"You can't fight us and win," one of the Elves said with amusement.

"Never know until you try," I told them and twirled my sword. Inside I was terrified, but I didn't want them to know that so I was borrowing Loki's ego for a moment.

They ran forward and Troy shot two of them in the chest. They screamed in pain and stumbled backwards and a third charged me. I sliced into his stomach and he bellowed as the blade burned his flesh. I cut them a few more times and managed to cut off one of their hands, but they were so much faster than me.

"Loki! Thor!" I yelled as I fought against them. Two ran at Troy and overpowered him, taking the gun from him. I tried to attack them, but they grabbed me and forced me to drop the sword.

"Alys!" Troy yelled.

"Let's go," one of the Elves said.

"Don't hurt him!" I demanded.

"We don't care about this pitiful mortal," the Elf holding me said. "We've got what we want."

I struggled against their hold, but they were too strong. If only I had powers like the Aesir. If only I wasn't a mortal. Before I could say anything else to Troy, they transported me to Svartálfaheimr. It was a cold and desolate place that was fitting to the cold, heartless Dark Elves. I felt the coldness creeping into my body and before I could gasp, they chained me to a wall and the frost covered me and froze me in place. They didn't speak to me and as one, left me alone in the room. The room had one door on each side and there were no windows to let in any light or warmth. It was dark, musky, and cold and it felt too much like a tomb for my comfort.

The leader of the Dark Elves entered and stared at me. It was the one who had come to Asgard. "So, you're the mortal the

Aesir hold affection for? Why? What is it about you that makes you worthy of their attention? They've never given a mortal attention before or since. And how was it possible for you to resist my order?"

"I don't know," I whispered. I was actually hoping he knew how I was able to resist his order.

My breathing slowed, as did the beating of my heart. I was worried I would die, but the elves needed me alive. Didn't they? I hoped so. I really didn't want to die.

"You have a gift, I can sense it, but it's not anything strong. Why else then? Why would Odin bring a mortal to Asgard?"

"You're asking the wrong person," I told him slowly as I worked to get each word out. "He never explained why I was brought to Asgard. He never told me anything other than my parents were killed and he didn't want me to die too." My chest hurt. It hurt to talk. It hurt just to breathe in this cold.

"This is a quandary indeed," he said and seemed highly amused.

"Why is this a quandary?" I asked.

"Because I can't kill you or we lose you as our bargaining chip and it would just incur their wrath, but I feel that I shouldn't keep you alive either. If you are somehow special and I allow you to live, then you might come back and kill us or give the Aesir the power they need to rule over the nine worlds."

"I don't have a strong power. I don't have any power," I whispered to him.

"Lies."

"Truth. I was raised with them and beaten by Sif almost daily. I don't have any power. If I had power I wouldn't have taken the beatings." Even though I understood Sif now and I felt nothing towards her except friendship, I still would have gone back and protected myself better if I knew how.

"The girl doesn't even know her power. How amusing."

"I'm glad to be of service to you," I snarled.

"Oh, and she has a temper. That would most likely be from too much time with the Trickster."

"Or perhaps it's from living with the Aesir who will come here and slaughter you, so I know I have nothing to fear from you." I was actually terrified, but my death might be the best thing for everyone else.

He snarled and wrapped a hand around my throat. "You would be wise to keep your tongue in check. I might decide that I can keep your body hidden from them and end your life before I have to worry about what power you might hold."

"I don't have powers," I told him again. "I don't know why you think I do, but I don't." I wasn't sure where my mental strength was coming from because I would have thought I would be a sniveling wreck at the moment, but instead I just met his gaze. Could it be from Loki's darkness? Was it allowing me to be so bold and strong?

He released me and said, "We'll see what the future holds for you, Alys of Asgard."

I relaxed and wished that Loki was here with his flames to heat me up. Or that I could be back on the couch with Troy. Poor Troy must be frantic right now with no way to find me or travel across the worlds. Hopefully Loki and Thor wouldn't kill him for failing to protect me. I felt the darkness calling to me and wondered what it could do. Could it help me escape? Or would accessing it while confined just allow it to take over? And even if I broke free of this freezing wall, what then? I couldn't win in a fight against the Dark Elves. Plus, I had no way of returning to Midgard or even Asgard. What if the Aesir refused to meet their demands and I died here? I didn't want to die alone. I didn't want to die at all. I still had so much of my life left and yet here I was chained to a wall in Svartálfaheimr when I should have been cuddling with Troy on Midgard.

"You seem sad," a Dark Elf whispered as he approached from my left. He was much smaller than the leader, but there was no mistaking the darkness that consumed him. "Don't worry girl, we won't harm you, unless the Aesir try to play hardball."

"They'll kill you," I whispered.

"They won't attack us and risk your death. They'll meet our demands to get you back."

"They'll attack you and if you kill me, they'll torture you."

"You seem pretty sure of yourself. How do you know these gods will even care what happens to a single mortal?"

"Because I'm Alys of Asgard," I told him, "and my father will come for me."

"Your father? Odin is not your father, girl. You're born of two Midgard mortals."

"He raised me and he claimed me as his own. That means more than who I was birthed from."

"You don't know how long I have waited to hear those words," Odin said from behind the Elf. He killed the Elf before he even turned around and walked up to me. "Daughter, what have they done to you?"

"Told me I needed to chill out until you came," I joked.

He waved his hand and the ice disappeared, freeing me from the wall. I collapsed into his arms and he pulled off the wolf pelt he wore around his shoulders to wrap around me. "Are you injured?" he asked.

"No, just cold and very tired."

"Here, give me the child," Jord ordered Odin. He obeyed, handing me over to the goddess who was scowling. "I'm very upset with you, Alys."

"I'm sorry, Jord," I whispered.

"Lectures later, Mother," Thor said. "We need to get her to safety."

"Thor!" I called happily, although with a weak voice.

He smiled at me and asked, "Did you think I wouldn't come for you?"

"I thought you might be beating up Troy for failing to protect me."

"We contemplated it," Loki said. "But what could a mortal do against a Dark Elf? We knew that it was simply beyond his abilities."

"Plus, it would have wasted time that we could have used to find you," Thor added.

"How did you find me?" I asked the group of gods in the room with me.

"I had a vision," Heimdall said as he stepped into the room carrying the head of a Dark Elf.

"Heimdall," I greeted him cheerfully. I realized that greeting a friend warmly while he held another being's head was not something the mortals would consider sane

"Lie still so I can heal you," Jord ordered me. She pressed her hands to my chest and warmth began to seep into my body.

"What kind of vision?" I asked him.

"I saw you hanging in chains in a dungeon and a Dark Elf torturing you."

"Thankfully that wasn't happening yet," I muttered. I didn't think I could have survived the cold *and* torture.

"Although the wrath that would have caused from The All Father would have been something glorious to witness," Jord said with a smile.

"Why aren't you out there fighting them?" I asked.

"The others are fighting them. We came to secure you," Loki said. It seemed odd that they would all come to find me if they knew where I was and we all knew that it didn't require more than one or two of them at most to rescue me.

"Did you know that the humans have a movie where Thor is

part of a team that protects Midgard and Loki is a bad guy who keeps trying to usurp Odin? And Heimdall is a very *very* dark-skinned man?" I asked them all.

Heimdall laughed loudly. "Dark-skinned? How could that detail have been so wrong?"

I shrugged. "Not sure."

"And why would I try to usurp Odin? I don't want to rule Asgard. Do you know how tedious that is?" Loki asked with a look of disgust on his face.

"No, you would rather go off and start wars for me to try to stop and give me work," Odin said with a scowl.

"A team to protect Midgard, huh? That sounds boring," Thor said.

"In the movie, there are lots of bad guys with superpowers like you gods. I didn't get to finish the movie because the Dark Elves attacked, but it was pretty good. Thor and Loki were very handsome."

Thor and Loki straightened their shoulders and Jord laughed softly next to me. "Of course they would be handsome. Our boys are very handsome."

"And what about me?" Sif asked as she walked into the room splattered with black blood and holding a blade that dripped with Dark Elf gore.

"You're described as the Goddess of War and fight alongside Thor to help him with his..." I stopped talking because I realized what happened in the movie was too close to comfort. Thor dating a mortal caused issues with him in Asgard. It felt like confirmation that we couldn't be together.

"Help me with what?" Thor asked.

"Help you protect someone," I said vaguely.

"I might have to watch this...*movie*," Thor said.

"Children," Odin said, "let's focus."

"Yes, let's go kick some Dark Elf butt!" I yelled. They

looked at me quizzically and I amended, "You should kick some Dark Elf butt."

"Midgard has the oddest phrases," Sif whispered.

"You don't know the half of it," I told her with a soft laugh.

My body was about halfway warm and I smiled appreciatively at Jord. "Are you certain that you won't come home?" she asked me.

I set my hand on top of hers and said, "You were the mother I never had and while in my perfect dream I would stay with you all forever, it is time for me to go to Midgard where I belong."

"Are you happy there?" she asked me.

I nodded my head. "I've made friends already and a man is courting me."

"A man is courting you already?" she asked in shock.

"Things move quickly in Midgard because our lives are so short," I reminded her.

"It is a different world after all." She sighed and then looked at me seriously, "If you marry a Midgard man, you must invite us."

"Invite the Norse Gods to Midgard for the wedding?" I asked her with wide eyes.

She nodded her head insistently. "Yes."

"I don't know if the people of Midgard could handle all of you there," I told her honestly.

"They'll have to. I refuse to allow a Daughter of Asgard to be married without her family there," she told me adamantly.

"Very well, Jord."

"Good."

"I think she's a little young to discuss marriage yet," Odin said angrily.

"She wasn't discussing marriage, but I had to ensure she knew my wishes beforehand," Jord told him.

"How's the battle outside?" Thor asked Sif.

"Over with. They have the leader waiting for Odin's punishment."

"Over so quickly?" I asked her in shock. "I thought you were all worried about them and their strength? I thought you said those on Alfheim wouldn't be able to defeat them."

"It would seem we were wrong about their strength. Either that or they're hiding the rest of their army somewhere else. That makes no sense, though, since we're wiping out this part of their army and its leader," Thor said.

"Let's go speak to this leader," Odin said to the room with a smirk. Odin walked out of the room with Sif and Thor following closely behind. Loki hadn't spoken or moved since I mentioned courting Troy.

"Loki," I whispered. "Will you come hold my hand?"

His shoulders tensed, but after a moment he came and sat on the other side of me, picked up my hand, and held it in his lap. "How are you feeling?"

"I'm still cold, but Jord is working on it."

"I sense the darkness stirring in you," he whispered and stroked his thumb across the back of my hand.

"It tried to get me to use it to escape when I was chained to the wall, but I was afraid I wouldn't be able to free myself from the darkness' hold and it would just take me over, so I didn't use it."

He paused a moment as he looked at me. "That was a very smart decision," he whispered and resumed rubbing his thumb across the back of my hand again.

I closed my eyes and relaxed as I was healed and enjoyed what would most likely be my last moments with Loki. He seemed to feel the same and after a few minutes he moved so that I was resting with my head in his lap, which was infinitely more comfortable. He stroked my hair and I could feel his darkness being pushed further and further down while more light grew at the top. I was worried for a moment that he was taking more of mine, but he was simply creating his own.

"You are a very special person," Jord whispered to me. "There are very few beings who have the ability to grant light to another."

"I thought it was just because of the love we have for each other," I whispered to her. "Are you telling me that I'm actually creating it?"

She smiled and said, "No, you are creating it within him. Your love for him is accelerating it, but you have the ability to grant light to any creature. It's a very rare ability."

"So, this was the gift that the leader was talking about," I whispered in shock.

"He sensed it in you?" Jord asked. I nodded my head. "Most likely because they are a dark race and there is no light within them. It must have been frightening to be near you and not know what you could do."

"Could she give them light and turn them?" Loki asked.

Jord nodded her head. "Yes. In the old days, a being such as her would be taken to a temple and protected for the rest of her life. People would travel from all over just to be granted a moment of time with her."

"I don't want to live in a temple," I complained.

She smiled. "We won't be doing that to you. Midgard will be safe enough for you because none there have any of the gifts now."

"They used to though, didn't they?" I asked.

She nodded her head. "There was a time when those with gifts outnumbered those without. The Midgardians grew too greedy and obsessed with power and eventually killed each other off and the gifts faded away."

"How come I have this gift?" I asked.

She looked away from me and said, "I believe Odin felt it and that is part of why he brought you to Asgard."

"He never mentioned it to me."

"It is not my place to speak for the All Father," Jord whispered and I knew that was her way of telling me to drop that topic of conversation.

"Can I give a being light from afar?" I asked her.

Loki looked down at me and I knew he understood what I was asking.

"It would have to be someone you are connected with, but yes, it is possible."

"You really are my light," he whispered to me.

"And I will provide it to you even from Midgard."

"Will you not allow me to see you?" he asked me angrily.

"I would not deny any of you from visiting, but I only ask that you limit your visits."

"How much will you make me limit it to?"

"Do you really want me to give you a specific number?" I asked in shock.

"Yes."

"What is the point of me living on Midgard if you still visit me every day or every week?" I asked him angrily.

"Alys."

"Once a month at the most," I finally decided.

"That's not very often," he whispered.

"You should be spending your time finding a goddess to court," I told him.

"And what restriction will you give Thor?" he asked me as though I would give Thor a different option.

"He has the same restrictions as you."

"What of Odin?"

"Odin, Jord, and Heimdall do not have restrictions. Only you and Thor have the restrictions."

"Why? Why do we have to be restricted from seeing you?" he asked me and his body began to heat with his anger.

"Because we must learn to love others and if we see each other more often, then our love would never fade or allow us to move on," I explained sadly.

"My love for you will never fade," he told me sternly.

"It must," I whispered. "Or Asgard and the Aesir are doomed."

"What would you have me do?" he asked. "Would you have me forget you and find a woman to replace you?"

"Loki," Jord chastised. "She never said you had to forget her or that she wanted to forget you."

"She already did once," he snapped.

"Part of me never did. I still felt connected to you when you visited me. I felt like I knew you and I felt safe with you even when I did not know who you were." I admitted.

"What if I don't want to marry some goddess? What if I don't want to marry?" Loki asked.

"You need a goddess," I told him. "I feel it in my core that you are meant to be with a goddess and have powerful children."

"And will you have children with a mortal?" he asked me.

I shook my head. "No. I will not bear children."

Jord and Loki looked at me in shock and Jord asked, "Why not?"

"It is something I discovered that I do not want to experience. I can't really explain why, but I just know that I shouldn't have kids, or that I won't at least."

"What if the man who courts you wants them?" Loki asked.

"Then I am not the right woman for him," I said adamantly.

"It's time to send you home," Odin said as he reentered the room.

Loki bent down and kissed my forehead. He whispered,

"My love will never fade and I will carry your light within me always."

"Will you visit me next month?" I asked him. I shouldn't have asked him to visit me so soon, but I needed to see him to make sure we kept his darkness at bay. He nodded his head and helped me stand up. I hugged him tightly and kissed his cheek. "I'll see you next month."

"This battle was over too quickly," Sif complained and pouted while swinging her sword.

"There will be more battles," Odin promised her.

"Goodbye everyone, until we meet again," I said to them.

They placed their fists over their hearts and bowed to me as one, a symbol of respect that was normally reserved for Odin. I looked at him in shock, but he was bowing with them. He set his hand on my shoulder and in a flash of light, I returned to Midgard and Troy's living room.

CHAPTER NINE

"Alys!" Troy gasped in shock when I appeared in the middle of his living room. He stood up from the couch where he had been sitting.

Odin hugged me and whispered, "I will visit you soon, Daughter."

"Thank you for saving me today," I said sincerely. I would not have survived if they hadn't shown up.

"Who is he?" Troy asked me with a scowl on his face. He looked like he was angry with Odin. Why? Was it because he was showing me affection and Troy didn't know who he was?

"Troy, this is the All Father, Odin, King of the Aesir and Ruler of Asgard," I introduced. "And my adoptive father."

"You must be Troy, the one who has been kind to Alys. You have my deepest gratitude and I grant you this gift." Before Troy could move away, Odin placed his hand on Troy's head and light flashed all around him. "Use it wisely."

Odin disappeared and Troy looked at me in shock. "What was that?"

I shrugged. "He gave you some type of gift. He didn't specify what it was. Do you feel different?"

He stretched his arms and then looked at me in shock. "I think he made me stronger and faster."

"Really?" I asked in shock. "Odin hasn't gifted a mortal with those powers in centuries."

"Are you alright?" he asked me as he set the discussion about his powers to the side. "Did they hurt you?"

"Just a little freezing, but Jord healed me," I explained as he hugged me.

"I was so scared that they would hurt you and I had no idea where you were or how to find you. Then Thor and Loki came and they refused to tell me anything," he explained.

"They took me to another world called Svartálfaheimr," I explained to him. "And no, there would be no way for you to travel there."

He kissed me deeply and whispered, "I was really worried about you."

I smiled and felt happiness within me knowing he had been worried about my safety. Did it make me a terrible person to turn away two gods who had very recently been courting me and already have a new man courting me here?

"Will they come again?" he asked.

I shook my head. "The Dark Elves have been taken care of."

"I meant the Norse Gods."

"Oh, well yes. They have told me that they will visit me from time to time, but I expressed my desire for Thor and Loki to visit infrequently."

"Why?" he asked.

"Because I don't want them trying to keep me from dating men here on Midgard," I explained softly.

"And they agreed to that?" he asked doubtfully.

"I gave them no other alternative. That was the stipulation to them visiting me. End of story."

"I bet they didn't just say 'yes' to your stipulation," he said and stared at me expectantly.

"No, but they will abide by it," I assured him.

"So, you really dumped two Norse Gods to date men on Midgard?" he asked.

"As crazy as it sounds to you, yes. I'm supposed to be here and this is the place I am supposed to find a man to court me from."

"So, are we still on for dinner tonight?" he asked.

What?

"Tonight? I was gone a whole day?" I had forgotten time was different on the other worlds.

"Yes, would you rather not go? We could postpone..."

"No, I want to go," I said seriously, "it's our first date. I can't miss it."

"Then we should get changed," he said with a smile.

I whispered, "I'm sorry if you were worried about me."

"All that matters is that you are safe and back here with me."

"I better hurry and change," I told him and ran up the stairs to my room. If it weren't for Jord's healing I would be exhausted, but I felt fully recovered and awake. I changed into a dress and painted my eyelids and lips and then stared at my reflection. I looked so different than I usually did on Asgard. Would I really be okay here on Midgard? Was going out with Troy a smart decision? At least he knew about the gods already so I didn't have to hide it from him when they came to visit. It made things a lot easier on that front. Perhaps it was too soon to settle on one man when I had just arrived. I shook my head and scolded myself. I wasn't marrying Troy tonight, just going on a date. I took a deep breath and then walked down the stairs where Troy was waiting for me wearing very nice-looking clothes.

"You look gorgeous," he whispered.

"Thank you. You look handsome as always."

He opened the door for me and we walked to his car. Once we were buckled and driving I said, "You're handling all of this pretty well."

He smiled and said, "I may or may not have had interactions with gods before."

"What!" I demanded in shock.

"That is a discussion we will have another day."

"You're just going to drop that bomb on me and expect me to wait to find out the story?"

"Yep."

"You can't do that!" I paused and then asked softly, "Are you a god?" That would ruin everything with Thor and Loki. If he was a god they would never forgive me for turning them down and letting Troy court me.

He laughed and shook his head. "No. Odin would have been able to tell if I was a god when he granted me these gifts."

"Why didn't you tell me?" I asked softly. I felt betrayed a bit and lied to with his omission of this information.

"Again, that is something we will have to discuss later. Tonight, is not the night for that topic."

"Are you from Midgard?" I asked fearfully. Whether he wanted to talk about it or not, I needed to know.

"Born and raised here," he said with a nod.

That didn't actually answer my question, but he obviously did not want to discuss this tonight so I would wait until tomorrow and then hound him until he answered me. If he didn't answer me, I would have to leave.

"What about Drake? Has he encountered gods before?" I asked.

"Yes."

I turned and faced out the window angrily. How could they have kept this from me? How come they didn't tell me? What if he was actually working with the Dark Elves? I glanced at him and wished I was able to carry Loki's sword with me.

"Why are you looking at me like that?" he asked me quietly.

"Did you know the Dark Elves were going to show up at the theater?" I asked him nervously.

He turned to look at me with wide eyes and then turned back to face the road as he drove. "Of course not. I never would have put you in danger like that."

"Do you know about my gift?" I asked even quieter. My body was tense, ready for a fight or to escape. It didn't matter how I felt about him, if he was a danger to me I would run.

"Yes, but it's not what you think," he said quickly. "I know of it and have heard stories about it, but I don't have a use for it or desire to use it."

"So, you wouldn't try to use me to gain power or money?" I asked him.

Or lock me in a temple somewhere? Or sell me to the highest bidder?

He pulled over, turned the car off, and turned sideways to face me. "I would never do any of that," he said seriously. "If I had wanted to, I definitely would have done it in the beginning. I have no ill will towards you, Alys. And I have been completely honest about my affection for you."

"Do you have a gift aside from what Odin granted you?"

He smirked. "Yes."

"What is it?"

"These are the things that you have to learn as you date," he told me.

"These are things that I need to know to stay safe," I said angrily. "Were you actually capable of defeating the Dark Elves?" I knew my darkness was taking over, but at the moment I didn't care.

"No, I was not capable of defeating the Dark Elves that

attacked at the theater. Perhaps now with added strength I might be able to, but I highly doubt it."

"Why are you being so secretive with me? I told you everything about me even though you could have chosen to think I was just crazy and sent me away." My anger was growing and I felt my light being pushed down by the darkness. "I should have known then that you weren't a normal Midgardian. I should have known that you were different somehow."

"I want you to make your decisions about me one piece at a time. If I tell you everything at once it will be a lot to process and you might decide to make a rash decision, especially with the darkness that you took from Loki."

"So, you don't trust me? You think I'm too stupid and simpleminded to understand your situation. Did you forget where I came from?" My body vibrated with anger now and I wanted to hit something. Darkness began to tint the edge of my vision. If I wasn't careful, the darkness could completely take control of me. I had no idea what it would do. I had no idea what I was capable of.

"I do trust you and I like you very much, which is why I have told you as much as I have so far. Please, trust me. I promise that I will reveal it all to you shortly. Okay?"

I took a deep breath and pushed the darkness down. It was hard and the darkness tried to fight me, but I succeeded and I tried to compress it into a smaller size. "Fine." It wasn't fine, but obviously I wouldn't get anything more from him.

"Can we go in for dinner?" he asked me.

I nodded my head. The streets were busy, a large amount of people walking around, and the restaurant we went into was full. Why were so many people in one restaurant? There were a ton of different places to eat very close by. What made this place better? Troy walked up to the hostess and she smiled and talked with him like they knew each other. After a moment, she showed us to a table, much to the annoyance of the other patrons who were waiting for seats before us. Troy pushed in my chair for me and kissed my cheek before walking around to his seat. I picked up the menu and couldn't decide what to eat since most of it were things I had yet to try. I set it down and looked around at the restaurant. It was beautifully decorated in red and white and there was soft music playing in the background.

"Do you know what you want to eat?" he asked me after he set his menu down on the table.

I shook my head. "Could you order for me? I'm not sure what most of the items are."

"Of course," he agreed with a wide smile.

"Do you eat here often?" I asked him as I glanced at the hostess walking by with another couple to take them to their table. She was beautiful and had an amazing figure that she didn't try to hide in a form fitting dress.

"No, but I worked here when I was younger, so sometimes I come back because they have the best food in town. They're just more expensive than my budget allows."

What was his gift? If he wasn't fast or strong or had the same gift as me, then what was it? I hadn't seen him use his powers yet while living with him. What could they be?

"You're scowling at me," he commented.

"I'm thinking about you," I explained.

"Scowling while thinking about me is not a good sign," he said.

"I'm trying to figure out your gift."

He sighed. "I shouldn't have said anything about it."

"No, you should have said something sooner."

"This isn't how I was hoping our first date would go," he said sadly.

"Me neither."

"Then can't we just drop it and enjoy being together right now? You could have been killed and we could have never gotten this moment to enjoy."

He was right. "Fine, but I demand an explanation tomorrow from both you and Drake."

"Alright." I was far from alright, but I didn't want to ruin our first date. This was supposed to be an important day and even though I wanted to know about him, he was right. I could be dead right now and this date might never have happened.

"When do you go back to work?" I asked him to change the subject.

"In two days," he said sadly.

"Why are you sad about that?"

"I don't want to leave you alone. If something happens, I might not know until I come home and I wouldn't have any idea what to do."

"Were you worried when the Dark Elves kidnapped me?"

"Yes. I had no idea where they took you to or how I could get there."

"You wouldn't be able to get there," I said simply.

"Thor and Loki can travel between worlds freely, though?" he asked.

I nodded my head. "The Aesir are one of the few races with the ability to travel across the Bifrost."

"Can you use it?"

I shook my head.

"What happened while you were there?" he asked me softly.

"They chained me to a wall and froze me to it. Luckily, Heimdall had a vision about it so they were able to rescue me quickly and I managed to avoid the torture he foresaw."

"Chained you to a wall?" he asked in shock and then fury contorted his face. "Did they hurt you?"

"No, just made things a tad chilly and slowed my heart a bit."

"They could have killed you that way."

"I know, but lucky for me they didn't."

"Who rescued you?"

"Odin arrived first, then Jord who began healing me, and then the rest came."

"Thor and Loki?"

"They did as well."

"You love them?"

This was not where I had wanted this conversation to go. I was trying to turn things towards him and talk about something else. "Part of me always will, but our paths are not meant to be entwined in that manner."

"Do you wish it were different?" he asked with clenched fists resting on top of the table.

"Does it matter? I made my choice."

"It does."

I sighed. "I grew up wishing to be a bride for one of them, but when I realized that the truth of the matter was they should be with a goddess, I pushed the thought out of my head."

"They kissed you."

"Yes."

"They want you."

"Yes."

"But you turned them down?"

"Yes."

"You turned down two of the most powerful gods in existence to live on Midgard and to find a mortal man for a husband?"

"Yes."

"Do you know how insane that sounds?"

Hadn't we already gone over all of this?

"I do."

"Most wouldn't care about the consequences or the balance."

"Most perhaps, but I care. I would rather protect my family than live a dream life."

"So you would rather punish yourself than allow yourself to be happy?"

"It's not punishment. I should not have been on Asgard to begin with. I don't know why Odin brought me there and I am thankful and happy for the days I spent there, but Midgard is my rightful place."

"If they asked you to go back in the future, would you?"

"No."

"You would never move back to Asgard? Not even if Thor and Loki had wives?"

"No, I wouldn't want to be alone there. Here I can find a husband and live with him. There I would live alone and have to watch them have children and have each other."

"Do you want children?"

Wasn't it a bit early to discuss that? "No, I don't."

"Really?" he asked in shock and leaned back in his chair.

"I decided that I don't want children. Is that a problem for you?" I asked him.

He frowned a moment and then said, "Honestly, I never thought of myself having children. Even when I pictured being married, it never involved kids."

"Well, I know it's early in our relationship, but if we stayed together that is something that I'm not going to change my mind about. So, if you want children then perhaps we aren't meant to be a couple."

He smiled. "Well luckily for me, I don't plan on having them so for now, I get to keep you."

"For now?"

"Until you decide there are plenty of other men on Midgard for you to date."

I laughed and our waiter chose that perfect moment to come over. Troy ordered for me and we ate the salads that were brought out along with some breadsticks.

I wasn't sure how, but part of me felt Loki's darkness growing. I closed my eyes and focused on the feeling of him and sent him light. I wasn't sure how I knew to do it or how it even worked, but after a moment I felt him grow brighter and the darkness slink away from the new light.

I opened my eyes and found Troy staring at me in shock. "You just used your powers."

I nodded my head. "How did you know?"

"You glowed," he whispered.

I looked around the restaurant, but no one else seemed to notice. "Sorry, I didn't know you could tell when I was using it."

"Why did you just use it?"

"I felt the darkness growing in Loki."

"You can feel him from here?"

"I can feel everyone I am connected to," I whispered, "even you."

"You can feel me?"

"I can feel your energy and the light and darkness that you carry."

He cringed. "That's not something I wish you to see."

"You carry as much darkness as I do," I whispered.

"Only because you took on some of Loki's."

"Perhaps. Or perhaps I always had it and I just let go some of my light and exposed it."

"It's not surprising that Loki's darkness would be growing right now," he whispered.

"What? Why is that?"

"You left him. He loves you and he told you that he loves

you and you still left him to live on a completely different world and even gave him a restriction on when he could see you. That would cause darkness in any man."

I hadn't thought about all of that. I felt terrible, but I couldn't change my mind now. If there was only a way for me to ease his pain, I would. "Do you think poorly of me for my decision?" I asked Troy softly. I couldn't look at him so I looked at my hands on the table instead.

He reached across and took my hand in his. "How could I think poorly of you when your decision gives me the chance to get to know you and to date you?"

Our food came out and we didn't talk much as we ate. I felt comfortable around Troy, but I was still worried about what he needed to tell me. Could they be children of gods? There were some who on occasion lay with a mortal of Midgard. Or was he just gifted like I was? Maybe his gift was something silly so he was embarrassed to show me.

"Let's go," he said with a smile and held out his hand. I let him take my hand and instead of going to the car he led me to a shop a few blocks down the street.

"What is this?" I asked curiously.

"This is a dessert shop."

"Sugary desserts?" I asked nervously. I wasn't too big on those yet.

"Don't worry, this isn't that sugary." He opened the door and let me walk in ahead of him. There were a ton of different types of desserts. I looked at each one and read the names with increasing interest. Troy ordered for us and the man behind the counter put something in a bag and then handed him two small cartons of milk. "Let's sit over there," Troy suggested and pointed towards an empty booth in the back. I sat down in the booth and he sat across from me. He set one of the milks in front of me and took out a brown cookie with piece of chocolate in it.

"This is a chocolate chip cookie and is considered a favorite treat here."

I took it from him and bit into it. It was sweet, but very good as well. He opened the milk and I took a drink. The milk cut down on the sweetness and made it a perfect dessert. "This is wonderful," I said honestly and took another bite.

"I'm glad that you like it so much."

"Thank you for our date tonight."

He leaned forward and kissed me lightly on the cheek. "Thank you for agreeing to go on a date with me."

"I'm sorry for my behavior earlier."

"There's nothing to apologize for."

"This darkness is going to take a bit of time to adjust to," I admitted.

"We can learn to handle it together," he suggested with a smile.

I nodded my head happily and finished my cookie. "What now?"

"Now we head home," he said cheerfully. Why was he so happy that our date was over? I was actually sad. He linked hands with me and we walked back to the car. The streets weren't as busy anymore and I was grateful for that. I didn't like being around so many people at one time. Troy opened my car door for me and shut it once I was inside. I remembered that being called manners or chivalry or something like that.

Once we were home and inside, he gently pushed me against the back of the door and kissed me deeply. "You are gorgeous," he whispered. "I am one lucky guy."

"And I think I should have waited until later to come over," Drake said from the couch.

Heat rushed to my cheeks and I felt incredibly embarrassed that he had watched us kiss. I squeezed around Troy and ran up the stairs to my room to change clothes.

"You could have warned me you were in here," Troy said angrily to Drake.

"You should have noticed that I was sitting on your couch. I'm not exactly a small person."

"You're right, I should have been more observant."

"I don't blame you. It would be hard to focus with a beautiful woman like that in front of me."

"What are you doing here?"

Part of me wanted to hide in the room so I wouldn't have to face Drake after he caught us kissing. I knew I would miss out on their conversations if I stayed here though. I jogged down the stairs and sat on the couch at the other end from Drake. "What's up, guys?"

"How was your date?" Drake asked me.

"It was good. I really like chocolate chip cookies and milk."

He laughed. "Everybody does."

"I need to learn to bake them," I said adamantly.

"You're going to make Troy fat," Drake warned me. "He's going to be eating sweets and good food and he won't know what to do with himself. He might actually have to start going running with me."

"I go running," Troy said defensively, "I just don't like running with you because you're always challenging me."

"You just can't keep up with me because you're so out of shape."

"I guess I'll have to start working out too," I whispered sadly.

"What?" Troy asked.

"I didn't have to work out on Asgard because the food was basically just enough to nourish me. It's hard to explain, but the food is almost magical in a sense and contains nutrients, but not anything extra. The only time people get fat there is if they drink too much mead and don't exercise. Food here is very fattening, though." I felt like I'd already gained some weight since being here and I really didn't like it.

"Did you talk to headquarters about that idea I suggested?" Drake asked Troy.

"I'm going to talk to them when I get back to work."

"What are you talking about?" I asked.

"Just work stuff," Troy said.

"If we break up and I can't work, I'm going to have to go live in the woods," I whispered to myself.

"No way!" Drake yelled. "If Troy ever lost his mind and broke up with you, you could just come live with me."

"We had one date and you're already talking about her living with you," Troy accused Drake.

"Hey, I'm not going to let one of my friends live in the woods just because you're an idiot." His comment made me smile. I liked knowing Drake considered me his friend.

"I didn't do anything, so you can't call me an idiot," Troy countered.

"Well, if you did, it would make you an idiot. And you don't have a great track record."

"I think it's time you two 'fessed up to your identities and what you know," I said with crossed arms, stopping their bickering.

Drake looked at me in shock and then looked at Troy and asked, "What did you tell her?"

"Nothing yet," he said with a scowl.

"You two are way too laid-back for coming into contact with beings who aren't from this world," I told them, "And I want answers."

Troy sat down and Drake heaved a heavy sigh. "There are some things we can't tell you," Drake started, "Because they're classified and..."

"Bullcrap," I said and interrupted him. "You tell me everything or I leave."

"Leave?" Troy asked in shock, his posture stiffening.

I nodded my head and gave him my serious look. "I'm not going to live with someone who withholds information from me."

"Where do we start?" Troy asked Drake.

"I don't know."

"How about you tell me what god you've met before," I said to Troy.

"Well, the first god I met was Odin when I was a child," Troy said, "but since then, I've met others from other religions."

"Other religions?" I asked him in shock. "What do you mean, *other* religions? There are other gods?"

"I've met Ares," Drake said.

"Who is that?" I asked softly.

"He is the God of War for the Greeks," Drake explained.

A God of War? I hadn't heard of this before. "Maybe it was an Aesir who just gave you a fake name," I suggested, even though I didn't even believe that.

"This is actually part of our job," Troy admitted. "We are supposed to contact all of these supernatural beings and find out their intentions towards Earth."

"I thought you were just a cop," I whispered.

He shook his head.

"So you didn't come to the hospital because it was part of your job?"

"No, we came because someone saw the Bifrost for a moment before you landed and I felt it connect with Earth," he whispered, "but at the time, we weren't sure what it was other than another world's transportation system."

I felt sick. Had everything been a lie? How could he feel the Bifrost?

"Alys," Troy whispered. "Are you alright? You look sick."

"You thought I was an alien," I whispered.

"No, the doctors tested your blood and confirmed you were human. We thought an alien had stolen you and erased your memory."

In a sense that was what happened.

"You didn't say anything to me about it," I reminded him.

"If they had erased your memory, I didn't want to expose their existence to you."

"Do these other gods live here?"

"Some."

Did Odin know? It didn't seem likely that he did. How could these beings have hidden themselves from them?

"Our job requires us to travel to their worlds from time to time," Drake told me, "Which is why sometimes we will be gone for more than a day."

"Have you been to the nine worlds?" I asked them.

They both shook their heads.

"We didn't know much about the Norse until you brought Thor and Loki here to fight the Dark Elves," Troy admitted.

"But you said you met Odin..."

"I didn't know who he was at the time. I didn't know until a few years later that it was Odin."

"How did you meet him?" I asked Troy.

"He's my father."

The world fell away. Troy was half Aesir. He was an heir to Asgard. Jord would be furious if she knew. How could Thor and Loki not have recognized his blood? How did Odin not?

"Alys!" Troy shouted, bringing me to the present.

"How come you don't have powers?" I asked. "Even half Aesir have powers."

"I have powers," he said, "but they're limited."

"How come Odin didn't recognize you?"

"I hid my aura from him," he admitted.

Being able to do that required a lot of power. "What powers do you have?" I asked him.

"I told you that I want you to learn about them as we date," he reminded me.

"Can you erase memories?" I asked him.

"No."

Good. I didn't need him messing with my memories when I didn't know.

"Why haven't you traveled to Asgard?" I asked him. If I had been half Aesir, I would have tried as soon as I could.

"I can't figure out which of the nine it is and I didn't want to travel to the wrong world," he admitted to me.

"Wait, you can travel on the Bifrost?" Drake asked him.

Troy shrugged. "I should be able to. I can sense it, but I haven't tried."

"Jord is going to freak out," I whispered. She hated when Odin had a mistress.

"Let's keep this between us for now," Troy suggested.

Could I hide this from them? This was big news. This was something Odin would want to know.

"What about you?" I asked Drake.

"I'm only a quarter god. My dad was half god from Orunmila, who is an Orisha of the Yoruba."

None of that made sense to me, but it meant there was another group of gods out there as well.

"So I'm the only normal one," I whispered and then laughed.

"No," Troy said. "You're half as well."

"No, I'm not. You even said the doctors confirmed I'm human," I reminded him.

"They can't detect when you are half," he informed me.

"So if you think I'm half, then whose am I?" I asked him angrily. There was no way that I was part god.

"We don't know. I think that you should ask Odin why he really took you to Asgard," Troy suggested.

Oh no, if I was Odin's that meant that Troy and I were siblings. No, I couldn't be Odin's because the others would have figured it out while I was on Asgard.

"I'm not Aesir," I whispered, "because they would have sensed that."

"No, but it means Odin wasn't truthful about what happened to your parents," Drake said softly, as if it would help lessen the blow that gave me.

This was too much. This was ridiculous. There was no way this was true. Had Odin betrayed my parents and stolen me?

A dark-skinned man appeared in the room and I could immediately see the resemblance between Drake and him. "Drake, we need to speak," the man said with a thick accent.

"Of course, Grandfather," Drake said and led him out to the backyard.

"Are you okay?" Troy asked me.

"No. No, I'm not. This is too much. This is insane. This is ridiculous."

"Why don't we summon Odin and have him confirm all of this and then we can move on from there," Troy suggested.

Part of me didn't want to know. Part of me wanted to stay in the dark about the truth to my past and what had happened to cause Odin to bring me to Asgard.

"Odin," I whispered.

He appeared in front of me and smiled warmly. "It hasn't even been a full day and you already miss me?"

"Odin," I whispered to him with shaking hands, "do you know this man?" I pointed to Troy and refused to look at him.

Odin looked at Troy and said, "He's the one you chose to live with here."

"Look closer," I told him. I don't know how I knew, but I felt it when Troy exposed his aura. It was like a warm, gentle wind against my skin.

Odin cursed and said, "I didn't know you were born."

"I know," Troy said. "My mother convinced me to hide myself from you."

"She told me she lost the baby," he explained.

"Odin, what happened to my parents?" I asked him. "Why did you bring me to Asgard?"

Odin looked up at the ceiling and I thought he wasn't going to tell me, but he took a deep breath and began. "Your father and I never got along. He would fight me whatever chance he got, but luckily, he couldn't travel to the Nine Worlds. When I was visiting Midgard one day, I happened upon him and his mistress and, as usual, we got into a fight. I ended up killing him and then his mistress attacked me. I was enraged and killed her as well. I immediately regretted my actions, but it was too late to do anything about it. It was only after the fight ended that I discovered you. I felt responsible for you and so I took you to Asgard with me. I couldn't bear to let you die because of my mistake."

He had killed my parents! My parents were dead.

"Who was my father?" I asked him.

"He was known as the God of the Sun and went by the name Apollo."

"That's why your gift is light," Troy whispered in shock.

I wanted it to be a lie. I wanted this to be false, but I felt it within my soul that it was the truth. "Why didn't you tell me?" I asked him. Why had he withheld it from me for so long?

"I was ashamed of myself for losing control. I am sorry, Alys. If I could change the past, I would."

"So, I'm not a Daughter of Asgard. I'm a daughter of...I don't even know what they call their place."

"Olympus," Troy said.

"No, even though your blood may not be Aesir, you are still the Daughter of Asgard. You still have our blessings and love," Odin said earnestly.

"Troy is a Son of Asgard," I whispered.

"He is," Odin nodded.

"At least we aren't related," Troy offered with a smile.

That was a good thing.

"I'm sorry," Odin said and took my hands in his. "I truly am."

Even though my heart felt broken and I felt betrayed, I couldn't fault Odin for withholding such information. I was still furious, but I held too much love for Odin to shun him.

"I believe you," I whispered.

Part of me wanted to scream at him and hit him, but I shoved it down. I would deal with these feelings later.

He hugged me and said, "Is there anything you want? Is there some way I can pay you for this?"

"Can you give me the ability to travel the Bifrost?" I asked him.

His eyebrows furrowed and he said, "No, but I can give Troy that ability."

"I already have it."

"I'll allow you one boon," Odin told me, "that you may take anytime you wish. Troy, you and I will speak later." He disappeared and I dropped to my knees on the ground.

Everything I knew was wrong. Everything I thought I knew was a lie. I didn't even know anything anymore. I had no knowledge of reality. My father had lied to me about everything. He had killed my true parents.

"It'll be alright, Alys," Troy whispered to me.

"Can you contact the Greeks?" I asked softly.

"That may not be wise," he said tentatively.

"Can you?" I asked again, more as a demand instead of as a request.

"Yes."

"I want to speak with them."

"I will contact them as soon as I get back to work," he said. "I don't have the ability to contact them right now."

"Apollo," I whispered softly. What were you like, Father? Were you a good god or an evil one? Surely the God of the Sun was good. Did he have a wife? If so, what would she think of me? What were the other gods like?

Drake walked inside and asked, "What happened?"

"Odin came," Troy said.

"You're alive, so that's a good sign," Drake said with a smile.

"She's part Greek," Troy told Drake instead of discussing the meeting with his father.

"Greek? Hm, that's interesting. We have more contact with them than the other gods, but they're still aloof."

"She wants to meet them."

"Which one? Definitely not Hera or Hades. Perhaps Zeus or even Hercules. I think Hercules is still on Earth."

Who were all of these people he was talking about? Were these my family members? Or my father's family members?

"We could start with Hercules. He'd be the most sympathetic to her," Troy agreed.

"He's also one of the more level-headed ones of the group. I think that's because he's half."

"Half?" I asked and tilted my head to the side.

"Hercules is half god like you. His father is Zeus, the leader of the Greek gods, and he lives on Earth."

"So, he's my brother? Or cousin?"

"He would be your uncle, actually. He and your father are half-brothers."

"The Greeks are quite the odd group when it comes to family relations," Drake said.

I closed my eyes and took a deep breath. "This is insane."

"It is a lot of change and information to take in," Troy agreed.

"You know they're going to want to talk to her," Drake told Troy.

"Who?"

"Our bosses," Drake said. "They'll want to interview you and get your information. At least this way you'll be able to get an ID and you will be able to work if you want to."

At least there was one plus to all of this craziness.

"Maybe they'll even offer you a job there," Drake suggested. "We have lots of openings and you seem smart."

I wasn't sure if that was a compliment or not.

"I'll take her in when I go back," Troy said.

"Will they lock me up?" I asked nervously. Some of those TV shows and movies I had watched portrayed humans as terrified of anything not like them and more apt to kill it or experiment on it than let it go free.

"No, they'll just talk with you and once they determine that you're not a threat to humanity, they will record your identity and give you ID and all of the documentation you need to live on Earth. They might even offer you a job, but I wouldn't get your hopes up about that. They will also take a piece of hair and some blood from you."

"Blood! Hair?" I asked in shock. "Why?"

"They keep records of all of us so that if we do commit a crime, they can figure out which one of us did it faster."

"How soon will I be able to meet my uncle?" I asked.

"It depends on if he is still on Earth or not. He visits the others on Mount Olympus from time to time. If he is there, then we will have to contact one of the others and I'm not really sure who I would contact."

"What about Artemis?" Drake suggested. "She's Apollo's twin sister."

"I haven't talked to her before," Troy said. "I don't know how she would react."

"Do you think they'll kill me?" I asked him.

"No. I'm more worried that they'll try to kidnap you," Troy admitted.

"That would go over well with the Norse," Drake said sarcastically.

"That could start a war," Troy said, "and that is not something that we want to happen. If Earth was caught in the crossfire of two groups of gods battling, it would mean a lot of human deaths and a lot of destruction."

"Has that happened before?" I asked curiously.

"Once and it destroyed a huge chunk of land and an entire civilization of people."

"Wow." That must have been some fight.

"From what I've heard, it was an incredible fight."

I realized something else and felt more sorrow filling me up. "Loki is not going to like that you're Odin's son," I whispered. I could already see the fury that knowledge would cause. For him to discover that I was allowing an Aesir to court me, whether he was half or not, would be a blow to him after the way I left. It wouldn't matter to him that Troy lived on Midgard. He would see it as me choosing Odin's son over him. It would be even worse than choosing Thor over him. Was there any way that I could explain it to him that would *not* cause him to freak out? Would he try to hurt Troy? Would Thor try to hurt him? Even though they were brothers, I was sure it would upset Thor. I had no idea how Thor would react to me courting his half-brother. I had a feeling that he would be about the same as Loki. I had to make sure that neither of them harmed Troy. The easiest way was to end our courting now.

"I was already thinking about that," Troy admitted. "Do you think they'll challenge me for you?" he asked. Strangely he didn't sound scared, only curious.

I sighed loudly. "I don't know. Maybe. Probably. They're going to be upset with me and think that I chose you over them already knowing that you were Odin's son. To them, it won't matter that you live on Midgard or that you're only half. To them, you will just be a Son of Odin. I wish I had some mead."

"Mead?" Troy asked in shock.

I nodded my head. "Mead calms me and allows me to forget about my worries."

"That's because it's alcohol and you get drunk on it," Drake said with a laugh.

"Well, apparently Asgard doesn't have drinking limits like we do," Troy said with a frown.

"We can't drink it until we turn twelve," I clarified, "and after that it is monitored. I'm not allowed to drink a lot of it without supervision. They also did that because I'm not a god." I laughed and said, "I wonder how Sif will take finding out that I'm half god."

"Do you think Jord will try to kill me?" Troy asked me.

I shook my head. "No, but she's going to be pissed at Odin. She might go on a hundred-year silent treatment again. Loki's father Laufey was joking about that one day and said the tension was so high around Asgard that people began begging her to talk to Odin just to ease the tension. She refused and wouldn't even stay in the same room with him for more than a few minutes. She still didn't completely forgive him and this may make it even worse. I wonder if we had married, if she would still have wanted to come. She said I had to invite her, but if I'm marrying her husband's son from another woman, I'm not sure she will actually come."

Troy looked sick.

I said, "I'm not putting a ring on your finger. I was just thinking about her request to be present at my wedding to whoever I marry and how that might change if it's Odin's son. Calm down. Our relationship is far from marriage." Even further once I let him down fully when we were alone.

He relaxed a bit and Drake said, "We've learned quite a few new things tonight. This has been enlightening."

"What did your grandfather want?" Troy asked him.

"He came to warn me about some impending war. He didn't really go into specifics, but he said it was going to be bad and I needed to watch out for it and protect myself."

"Odin and the Norse were talking about a war too," I told them. "I wonder if it's related."

Troy and Drake looked at each other in shock. "We'll have to let headquarters know," Troy said with worry.

Drake nodded his head.

After Drake left, I sat with Troy a moment in silence before I finally worked up my nerve. "Troy, I need to tell you something."

"Okay," he replied and faced me.

"I don't want to move too fast and I'm not certain what's going to happen now that I'm going to meet my blood family. I really do value your friendship, but..."

"But you don't want to be more than friends," he finished for me. "I figured this was going to happen."

"Are you mad?" I asked him.

He shook his head. "It hurts a bit, but I'll get over it."

"Still friends?" I asked.

He smiled and nodded. "Still friends."

CHAPTER TEN

As Troy drove, I felt my nerves growing more and more. I felt more nervous than I had the day I jumped from the top of the falls in Asgard, a jump that had nearly killed me. What was this place going to be like? What were the people there like? Would they hurt me even if Troy was there? Maybe they were going to lock me up and try to use me against the Norse.

Troy patted my leg reassuringly and said, "It'll be alright, Alys. I promise that they won't hurt you or try to hold you prisoner at headquarters."

Humans were so unpredictable, though. How could he possibly know that for certain?

We drove out of the city and out into the fields that stretched as far as I could see. Troy made a sudden left turn and I would have thought he had fallen asleep or gone crazy had we not turned onto a path that was already worn down by other vehicles driving this way. The grass grew tall enough that we couldn't see around us and anyone else wouldn't be able to see us driving through the field. We drove for several minutes and then in the distance I could see a fence with a man standing in front of it.

"Secret facility," I whispered in shock.

"This is headquarters. We have another facility in town that is out in plain sight. The humans just think that we're cops. Even the cops think we're cops from another branch."

He stopped at the fence and the man walked around to the driver's side window and asked, "How are you today, Agent Stevens?"

"Doing good. I'm bringing in a new face," Troy said and leaned back so the man could see me.

"Alright, head straight to check in."

Troy nodded his head and somehow the fence began opening. I didn't see anyone pushing it open, though. It had to be some type of electric power.

"So, how often to you bring in new people?" I asked him to try to take my mind off of the fear.

"Not that often. We're actually a rare breed, despite you stumbling into two of us."

That was actually reassuring. I didn't think I could handle a swarm of partial gods. We drove through the fence still through the tall grass and then a hundred feet later, the grass ended and a huge base stood. It looked like a military base with jets, helicopters, hummers, and all kinds of people running around. Troy drove up to the closest building and parked the car. I climbed out and followed him into the plain grey building. Inside was a long desk with a man sitting behind it and behind him was a single door.

"Agent Stevens reporting in," Troy said sternly to the man who looked half asleep.

The man stood up and smiled. "Stevens! It's been a while since I have seen you."

Troy tilted his head towards me. "Brought a new one in."

The man looked at me and his smile wilted. "A new one? I thought we had found them all."

"She just arrived a week ago," Troy explained.

The man had light skin, bright red hair and freckles all over. He seemed old, but his eyes were young and he moved with a lot of energy. "What's your name?" he asked me.

"Alys."

"Do you have a surname?" he asked.

I looked at Troy and he shook his head. "No."

"Alright. Do you know your birth date?"

"No, but I'm eighteen."

"Sex?"

I looked at Troy with wide eyes and he laughed softly. "He means what gender are you?"

"Female." Wasn't that obvious?

"Sometimes beings choose to look like a different gender on this planet," Troy explained.

"And what are you?" he asked me.

"Um, half Midgard...I mean half human and half god."

"She's from the Greeks," Troy added.

"The Greeks! Oh boy. That's going to be fun," he said with sarcasm.

"Is the Chief in?" Troy asked.

The man nodded his head. "I'll enter her information in while you head back. Welcome to Earth, Alys."

"Thanks," I muttered and followed Troy towards the door. There was a loud buzz and then the door opened. It must have been electronically activated too.

The door opened to a long hallway with lots of doors and not a single window in sight. Troy knocked on the fourth door on the left, one that looked like every other door there and all without markings.

"Enter," a man's deep voice said from inside.

Troy opened the door and nudged me forward with a hand on my lower back. "Sir, I've brought in Alys."

The man was a giant. He barely fit in the office and the desk he sat behind looked like it should belong to a child. Had they made a chair to fit him? He had a long beard and his eyes held age within them like Odin's.

"You're a Vanir," I realized in shock.

He smiled and Troy looked at me in shock. "You're the first person to know that with just a look," the Vanir said.

"I can sense it. I'm not exactly sure how, but the Vanir are slightly different than the Aesir and they're both much different than the Giants or Elves," I said as I tried my best to explain. Truthfully, I didn't understand it myself.

"Alys is from..."

"She's Odin's step-daughter," the Chief said with a smirk. "Alys, the mortal Daughter of Asgard."

"How'd you know that?" I asked him in disbelief. Even if he was Vanir, they didn't know everything that happened on Asgard.

"I visited Asgard after you were brought there," he explained.

"He real father was Apollo," Troy informed him.

The Chief's eyes widened and he exhaled loudly. "Well, that's interesting and possibly disastrous. How did you end up here?"

"I came to Midgard because this is where I belong, not on Asgard," I told him truthfully.

"Except that you might actually belong on Mount Olympus," the Chief said and stroked his long beard as he looked off in thought.

I looked at Troy and said, "I don't want to leave Midgard."

"We will discuss it with the Greeks," Troy assured me. "They let Hercules live here so I don't see why they wouldn't let you."

"Except for the fact that she's living with the son of the man who killed her father," Chief said sadly.

"But he isn't even associated with Asgard right now," I defended.

"It's just something we have to consider that they will be upset about," Troy said softly.

I didn't like where this was going. Not one bit!

"Take her down to get sorted out and send them contact," Chief ordered Troy. "Let's hope they're in a good mood."

"There's something else," Troy said.

"Oh?" Chief asked.

"Several of the groups are reporting an impending war," Troy informed him, "It worries me that the different factions would report the same thing."

"An impending war? With whom?"

"No one has said who the war will be between; just that it was going to happen and soon."

Chief leaned back in his chair, the springs groaning from his massive size, and sighed. "Every group has their apocalypse stories. I hope this isn't those."

"You mean like Ragnarok?" I asked with a lump in my throat.

He looked at me in shock. "You know about it?"

"Loki and Thor used to sneak me into the meetings without Odin knowing. Odin didn't want me to know because he thought my mortal mind wouldn't be able to handle it, but I wanted to know in case there was some way that I could help."

He smiled and said, "You are quite the woman, Alys."

"I doubt that it's Ragnarok," I told him. "All of the signs haven't happened."

"True," he mumbled. "There are so many other stories and none of them point to anything good, especially not for Earth."

"Could it be a battle between them?" I asked softly. Could I be the cause? Could it happen because the Greeks would want vengeance from the Norse?

"I don't think that's it," Chief said and shrugged, "but who knows. Every possibility must be discussed and a plan must be ready just in case."

"I'll put together a team," Troy said.

"Go get her set up and contact her lineage. We'll have a meeting soon to discuss this news."

Troy nodded his head once and led me out into the hallway. "You okay?" he asked me softly.

I nodded my head and explained, "I'm just worried about my family."

"The Norse or the Greeks?" he asked.

I sighed heavily. "This is going to get so confusing. I wish there was an easier way to discuss all of this."

He slipped an arm around my shoulders and squeezed. "It'll be alright. I'm here for you and so is Drake."

But would the Greeks let me stay by their sides? What if they demanded I come to their mountain? I was an adult, but I couldn't fight a god and I didn't have magical powers to keep myself here.

Troy opened the door at the end of the hallway and I stared in shock at the massive open building in front of us. The first half was made up of cubicles with low walls, while the second half had what looked like scientists in a lab. The right side had weird circular openings with markings around them and the left had a doorway that looked like an entrance to a prison with iron bars.

Troy led me towards the first cubicle and the young woman there smiled up at Troy. "Stevens," she said in a high-pitched, happy voice. "It's been too long."

"Can you get Alys started on her identity information?" he asked her without smiling back.

She looked at me and the smile disappeared. "Fill out this form," she instructed me and handed me a clipboard with a piece of paper on it. It had a lot of questions and I wasn't sure how to answer most of them.

"I'll help you fill it out," Troy offered and took the clipboard from me. The woman gave me a sour look and then turned her attention back to her computer. "Sorry about her, we went on a couple dates and she seemed to really like me, but I didn't feel the same towards her. She's probably going to be rude to you because of it."

"We aren't dating either," I reminded him.

He cringed, still not happy that I had broken it off with him. What else was I supposed to say to that? It's not like I was the reason Troy and her didn't work out.

He led me to some chairs I hadn't seen and we sat down. He filled in some of the information that he knew and then he asked, "Do you plan on staying at my house?"

"That is the plan for now," I said and felt bad for using him. Maybe I should see if Drake would let me live with him?

He wrote down some information and then checked a bunch of boxes. "How would you describe your power?"

"Uh, is there a better way to say 'light giver'?" I asked and then laughed. How would one describe filling someone else with light and taking their darkness?

"I'll see if there's someone here with a little more insight. Perhaps the Greeks will know more as well."

I watched the people moving around, doing their jobs, and felt incredibly out of place. Technology was everywhere and there seemed to be a permanent static hum. Troy reached over and rested his hand on my leg.

"It'll be okay," he whispered. "I know this is all new and strange to you, but you'll get used to it eventually."

"I have a headache," I admitted to him.

"We'll go see the doctors in a moment and I'll ask them to give you something for it," he told me and then kissed my forehead as he stood up to take the form to the woman who was now glaring at me as though her look alone could kill me.

She looked up at Troy and smiled sweetly and talked to him in what was no doubt flirtatiously. Perhaps it should have bothered me, but it didn't since he had made it clear that he didn't have feelings for her and I had broken it off with him. He hadn't fully accepted it though, obviously. She did something on her computer and then Troy waved at me to follow him. We walked to the back where the doctors were and one of them opened the door to his room. He was short with thick black hair and a dark brown complexion. His glasses made him look old, but his face didn't seem old.

"Welcome," he greeted me.

"Hello."

"Dr. Patnik, this is Alys. Alys, this is Dr. Patnik, the top scientist here."

"Oh, you're flattering me," the doctor said with a smile. "So, Alys, what are you?"

"Uh, what?"

"She's half human and half Greek," Troy explained for me.

I was glad he said something because I would have said Asgardian.

"Oh! It's been so long since we've had a demigod!" he said with excitement.

"A demi...what?" I asked.

"A demigod. Demi means half or partial and then add god and it means you're half or partially a god."

That made sense, but I still couldn't see myself as being part god. I was so weak compared to the others.

"We're going to take some blood, okay?" Dr. Patnik said with a kind smile.

"Will it hurt?" I asked Troy.

"Just a bit. Here, sit in this chair," he told me. I sat down and then he took my left hand. "If you don't watch, it hurts less."

"I wasn't planning on watching," I said which made Dr. Patnik and Troy laugh.

Dr. Patnik hummed as he washed his hands, put on gloves, and took out a few pieces that looked slightly terrifying.

"Did you know that when I first came here, Troy was a wild teenager who got so angry at me for taking his blood that he shattered all of the glass walls enclosing our labs here?" Dr. Patnik asked.

"I don't know much about Troy's past," I admitted sheepishly. Did it make me a bad person to be living with a man I barely knew?

"He's very secretive," Dr. Patnik agreed.

"Why was he mad that you took his blood?" I asked even though Troy was right next to me.

"Because I took part of him. He didn't understand that we were taking it to test for diseases or other things that could be hurting him."

"I apologized afterwards and cleaned it up," Troy told me.

"And got yelled at by Chief," Dr. Patnik said. "Okay a slight pinch..."

I felt a pinch in my inner elbow and hissed in pain. Troy rubbed the back of the hand he was holding and said, "I used to be a very angry person."

"Why?" I asked.

"Because I felt like my father had abandoned me. I knew logically that he didn't know about me because my mother had hidden it, but I felt like he should have known I existed. It was stupid and childish, but at the time I hadn't met any other demigods and I was very out of place."

"How did you end up here?" I asked him. I could understand why he felt abandoned. If Odin had known, he would have brought Troy to Asgard, I was sure of it.

"Drake found me and brought me in. He and I have been friends ever since."

"Now that is a scary man if you're on his bad side," Dr. Patnik said. "Okay, pulling it out now." More pain and then he put a cotton ball on the spot he had taken the blood from and a piece of tape over it. "Leave it on for an hour so it heals."

"Why do you think Drake is scary?" I asked Dr. Patnik.

"You've obviously never seen him mad," he said with a smirk. "He's a great warrior when he needs to be."

"Can you give her something for a headache?" Troy asked Dr. Patnik.

"Of course!" he said with a broad smile. He went to a cabinet and pulled out a vile of liquid, extracted some into a syringe and then without warning he stuck it into my arm and pushed the liquid in. "Your headache should be gone within a few minutes."

"Thanks," I mumbled as I rubbed my arm.

We left and Troy led me back towards the cubicles. "So, does this mean Drake or you could have defeated the Dark Elves?" I asked Troy when we were away from Dr. Patnik's lab room.

He sighed loudly. "If he had activated his powers, yes, but we can't use them in front of other humans."

"You told me that you couldn't have defeated them."

"Not in my human form."

"Human form? You have another form?"

"No, it's just what we refer to the state in which we conceal our power. When we release it, we call it demi-form."

"So you could have defeated them?"

"Possibly."

"I could have died," I told him angrily. "They were considering killing me instead of letting me live because of my power."

"Odin wouldn't have let you die."

"They had me chained to a wall and frozen!" I snapped at him.

He stopped walking and turned to face me. "I'm sorry, Alys. I couldn't expose myself to the humans. If I had, my cover would be blown and I would have had to relocate or go into hiding and I didn't want to do that. I had faith that Odin and the others would save you."

I couldn't believe what I was hearing. "And if they tried to take me again today? Would you still let them take me?" I asked softly.

"No," he answered immediately with clenched fists.

"Why is it different now?" I asked angrily. "You would still have to expose yourself."

"It's different now because now I wouldn't care if I was exposed. Now, I would rather let the humans see me than let you get hurt."

"What is different now than before?" I asked in quiet fury. The darkness stirred within me and tempted me with images of destruction that would satisfy the anger.

"Now I have feelings for you and the thought of you getting hurt infuriates me and makes me want to tear someone's head off," he whispered. "I'm sorry that I didn't protect you before, but you won't have to worry about that in the future. I regret not helping you now, but I can't change the past."

I was still mad, but hearing him admit his feelings for me made the rage simmer to irritation. He started walking again and I followed him to the woman who hated me for being with Troy. "Have you decided on a surname?" she asked me with a scowl.

"Odinsdottir," I told her and spelled it for her.

Troy looked at me in shock. "The Greeks won't like that. You should consider taking on a human surname."

I shook my head. "I may be genetically a Greek, but I was raised by Odin and the Norse and I owe them this respect at the very least." It wasn't much, but I knew Odin would appreciate the gesture and it would make him happy for a moment. Even if I was still hurt and unsure of our future relationship, knowing that he had killed my parents.

"He's right," the woman said softly and with a quivering voice. "You should consider taking a name like Smith or Johnson instead. The Greeks are easily angered."

"They don't get to decide my surname," I told them firmly. They might decide to take me from Midgard, but they wouldn't take my surname or the love I held for the Norse from me.

"You're certain?" she asked me.

"Yes," I said and stared straight into her eyes, daring her to make another comment.

"Okay," she said with a sigh, "but don't say I didn't warn you." She typed on her computer and then looked up at Troy. "Her documents will be ready in about twenty minutes."

"Thanks," he said and then led me towards the odd circular openings. "Let's see if we can get in contact with..."

"Troy!" A deep voice bellowed.

Troy and I stopped and turned to find a man at least six feet and six inches tall with broad shoulders and bulging muscles walking towards us. "Hercules," he said in shock. "What are you doing here?"

"I came to talk with Chief and he told me that you had something important to discuss with me," the man said. He was filled with light and only had a tiny bit of darkness within him. He looked at me and his eyes widened. "You. You're one of us."

How did he know?

I looked at Troy and he said, "Hercules is Zeus' son and he's the demigod we told you we would try to find. Hercules, this is Alys. She's Apollo's daughter."

Hercules walked around me slowly and reached out towards my face. I wasn't sure what he was going to do, but I held my ground and hoped he wasn't trying to harm me. He rested his fingers against my cheek and whispered, "You look so much like Apollo and Artemis. You're the light that was lost. We tried to locate you, but we couldn't."

"I was rescued and taken off Earth to be raised after my father was killed," I explained vaguely.

"I need to take you to Artemis and Zeus," he said urgently.

"I don't want to leave here," I told him. "I want to live here."

"I just want to take you to meet them," he explained.

I looked at Troy nervously. "Troy?" I asked softly.

"She's your aunt," he said, "And I think you should meet your father's sister to learn about him and the rest of your family."

"Can't you come?" I asked nervously.

He shook his head. "No. I can't. My blood prevents me from stepping foot on their ground." How was that possible if I was allowed on Asgard? Odin must have altered things for me to live there. How much had been altered because of my presence on Asgard? Had I opened the possibility of them getting attacked by non-Asgardians because of my presence? Would it be different now?

"I swear no harm will come to you," Hercules promised.

"Will you swear to return me here or to my home on Earth afterwards?" I asked him.

He smiled. "That's a pretty smart request for someone unfamiliar with the Greeks. Yes, I swear to bring you back to your home on Earth after meeting Artemis."

"Tonight," I amended firmly.

"Could we do tomorrow? I'm certain that Artemis will want

a lot of time with you and Zeus will want time as well." he asked me.

"Fine, tomorrow night at the latest," I agreed.

"Great!" Hercules said with a wide smile of perfect straight white teeth.

I was afraid to go, but I also knew that this was my blood family and it was important to meet them. I hugged Troy and whispered, "If my family comes, don't tell them where I am. I don't want them attacking the Greeks." He nodded his head. "And I'll be back soon."

He hugged me back and kissed my cheek. "Stay safe."

Hercules was scowling when I turned back around. He asked Troy, "Can we use your portal?"

Troy walked towards one of the strange circular things and when he approached, a panel rose from the ground. He typed into it and blue light filled the circle. "It's ready."

Hercules took my hand and said, "Come, let's go fill our family with joy at your return." I nodded my head and found myself smiling along with him. He led me into the portal and I glanced back to smile one last time at Troy, who looked sad.

We stepped through the blue light and out onto a terrace with blue sky and wispy clouds all around. "Welcome to Mount Olympus," Hercules said, "Home of the Greek Gods." We were so far above the cloud line that it looked like the ground from a plane, or at least the photos I had seen of that. Was this really a mountain somewhere or an alternate planet like Asgard?

"How do you get here aside from the portal?" I asked him.

"I can travel here with a thought because my father gifted me with that ability, but I can't bring others that way. They should give you the same gift once they've met you."

Did I want to visit Olympus? Would I visit it more than Asgard? What rift would that cause between Odin and the others? As much as it hurt to consider, perhaps it would be best to cut ties with the Norse.

He led me to the right, around a pillar that had been in the way and I gasped. There were several buildings, but in the center stood a massive stone building with six pillars on the front of it. Everything was paved with stone and it looked like glimmering pearls. The lands stretched as far as I could see and evenly spaced were distinctly different buildings. There were trees around the grounds and beautiful flowers everywhere, but the buildings had their own unique landscaping. Off in the distance it appeared that there were floating islands, but I couldn't be certain. There were also several strange creatures roaming around. He led me down a path and said, "Be wary of the edges, there are no rails and if you fell, you wouldn't survive."

That was not something I wanted to hear. I stayed closer to him and tightened my grip on his hand. He had to notice, but he didn't comment or look to confirm. A large horse with wings trotted up to Hercules and nudged his shoulder. "Hello, Pegasus," he said warmly to the winged-horse. "How have you been, old friend?" The horse nickered and made odd noises with its muzzle. "I'll catch up with you later," he promised it, "but I am on urgent business right now." Pegasus bobbed its head and flapped its wings to fly up into the sky. I covered my face with my free arm and held onto Hercules as the wind from its wings pressed against me.

"A friend of yours?" I asked him.

"He was a gift from my father when I was a child. He was like a friend to me when I lived up here."

"Why did you choose Earth?" I asked him.

"Because I wanted to help protect the mortals from the dangers that often left Olympus to go down there."

"So, you're a hero?" I asked in shock.

He shrugged. "Some call me that. I think as a demigod, it's my duty to keep balance between the gods and the mortals."

Was that what I was supposed to do? Was that why I felt so compelled to leave Asgard when I discovered I was ruining their balance?

We walked to the huge building and I stared in awe at the hand-carved designs. It must have taken someone a very long time to create this building alone. I walked up to one of the pillars and ran my fingers along the depictions of a great battle. I felt a connection to the story even though I wasn't fully sure what was happening in it.

"That's your father," Hercules whispered and pointed to the man in a chariot holding a spear. "His loss was greatly felt in Olympus and when we couldn't find you, the family went into a panic. We felt it within us that you weren't dead, but since you were lost to us, we had no idea where you were or what had happened to you. We feared the worst and feared that Apollo's loss had simply clouded our judgment about you. Artemis locked herself in solitude for several years to mourn her twin brother's loss and the loss of you. She will be overjoyed to meet you."

"What is she like?" I asked him.

"You'll see for yourself shortly."

"Will any of the others be unhappy with my return?" I asked and refused to move closer to the doors. I needed to know if my safety would be an issue inside the room. Not that I was likely capable of defending myself against a god who wanted to kill me, but I wanted to be prepared.

He sighed. "Our family is constantly squabbling with each other, but on this topic, I am certain. You are the lost child and your return will only be met with joy."

I hoped he was right. I also hoped they allowed me some freedom such as choosing where I wanted to live and who I wanted to date. I could definitely see them not wanting me to date a son of Odin. I shook my head to rid it of that thought. Troy and I would never be. *Could* never be.

"Ready?" he asked.

No.

I nodded my head and he pushed open the marble double doors. They swung opened to reveal what I presumed was a council room with large chairs that resembled thrones, a table with maps and different pieces for battle strategies, and people in each of the thrones. They vibrated with power and I felt small compared to them all. It was similar to being around the Norse, but they often reined it in when I was there so I wouldn't be overwhelmed.

"The Light of Olympus has returned," Hercules announced in a booming voice.

All heads turned to look at us and I really wished he hadn't made the announcement like that. A beautiful woman in a white dress with a hound at her side, rose quickly from her seat and walked as fast as one could without running to me. I didn't need to ask to know that this was my aunt, because her features were very similar to mine and she was the most moved by my return with tears brimming in her eyes.

She asked, "What is the name that you go by?"

"Alys," I whispered.

She hugged me tightly and said, "Welcome home, Alys. Your Aunt and the rest of your family have missed you. I am so happy for your return."

Thank you for reading my novel. I hope you enjoyed it.

MORE FROM CATHERINE BANKS

Calvin's Alien Adventure

Pirate Princess Trilogy
Pirate Princess
Princess Triumvirate
Pirate Queen*

Little Death Bringer Duology
Mercenary
Protector
Little Death Bringer, The Official Coloring Book

Her Royal Harem Series
Royally Entangled
Royally Exposed
Royally Elected
Royally Enraged
Her Royal Harem, The Complete Series
The Demon's Fair
Her Royal Harem, The Coloring Book

Zodiac Shifters Paranormal Romance Series
Centaur's Prize
Tiger Tears
Lion About

The Lioness's Harem Trilogy
Lonely Lioness

Anderelle: Minloa Trilogy
Queen of the Stars
Empress of the Galaxy
Goddess of the Universe

Demonic Contract
Anja's Secret
Daughter of Lions
Dragon's Blood
The Last Werewolf
Last Ama Princess
Transforming Rose
Lady Serra and the Draconian
Alys of Asgard
Phoenix Possessed
Sybil Deceived
The Pawn
Stone Heart
Of Sky and Sea

*COMING SOON

ABOUT THE AUTHOR

Catherine Banks is a USA Today bestselling fantasy author who writes in several fantasy subgenres under two pseudonyms. She began writing fiction at only four years old and finished her first full-length novel at the age of fifteen. She is married to her soulmate and best friend, Avery, who she has two amazing children with. After her full-time job, she reads books, plays video games, and watches anime shows and movies with her family to relax. Although she has lived in Northern California her entire life, she dreams of traveling around the world. Catherine is also C.E.O. of Turbo Kitten Industries™, a company with many hats including being a book publisher and Etsy store full of nerdy fun.

facebook.com/catherinebanksauthor

twitter.com/catherineebanks

amazon.com/author/catherinebanks

bookbub.com/authors/catherine-banks